I0836059

THE
RIVER OF LIFE

and other Stories

by

ALEXANDER KUPRIN

Translated from the Russian by

S. KOTELIANSKY AND J. M. MURRY

Fredonia Books
Amsterdam, The Netherlands

The River of Life and Other Stories

by
Alexander Kuprin

ISBN: 1-4101-0568-7

Reprinted from the 1916 edition

Fredonia Books
Amsterdam, The Netherlands
http://www.fredoniabooks.com

In order to make original editions of historical works available to scholars at an economical price, this facsimile of the original edition of 1916 is reproduced from the best available copy and has been digitally enhanced to improve legibility, but the text remains unaltered to retain historical authenticity.

INTRODUCTORY NOTE

Alexander Kuprin was born in 1870. He attended the Cadet School and the Military College at Moscow, and entered the Russian Army as a lieutenant in 1890. Seven years later he resigned his commission to devote himself to literature.

He achieved fame by a novel, *The Duel*, in which he described with a ruthless realism the army life in a garrison town upon the Western Frontier. The book, which in reality falls into line with the rest of his work as a severely objective presentation of a life which he has found vivid and rich, was, fortunately for his success, interpreted as an indictment of the Russian Army and the ill-starred Manchurian campaign. He was accepted by the propagandists as one of themselves, and though he protested vigorously against his unsought reputation, his position was thenceforward assured.

But the interest of Kuprin's talent is independent of the accidents of his material. He is an artist who has found life wide and rich and inexhaustible. He has been fascinated by the reality itself rather than by the problems with which it confronts a differently sensitive mind. Therefore he has not held himself aloof, but plunged into the riotous waters of the River of Life. He has swum with the stream and battled against it as the mood turned in him ; and he has emerged with stories of the joy he has found in his own eager acceptance. Thus Kuprin is alive as none of his contemporaries is alive, and his stories are stories told for the delight of the telling and of the tale. They may not be profound with the secrets of the universe ; but they are, within their compass, shaped by the perfect art of one to whom the telling of a story of life is an exercise of his whole being in complete harmony with the act of life itself.

J. M. M.

CONTENTS

I

THE RIVER OF LIFE

THE RIVER OF LIFE

I

THE landlady's room in the 'Serbia.' Yellow wallpaper; two windows with dirty muslin curtains; between them an oval squinting mirror, stuck at an angle of forty-five degrees, reflects a painted floor and chair legs; on the window-sills dusty, pimply cactuses; a cage with a canary hangs from the ceiling. The room is partitioned off by red screens of printed calico: the smaller part on the left is the bedroom of the landlady and her children; that on the right is blocked up with varied odds and ends of furniture—bedridden, rickety, and lame. In the corners all kinds of rubbish are in chaotic cobwebbed heaps: a sextant in a ginger leather case, and with it a tripod and a chain, some old trunks and boxes, a guitar without strings, hunting boots, a sewing machine, a 'Monopan' musical box, a camera, about five lamps, piles of books, dresses, bundles of linen, and a great many things besides. All these things had been detained at various times by the landlady for rent unpaid, or left behind by runaway lodgers. You cannot move in the room because of them.

The 'Serbia' is a third-rate hotel. Permanent lodgers are a rarity, and those are prostitutes. Mostly they are casual passengers who float up to town on the Dnieper: small farmers, Jewish commission agents, distant provincials, pilgrims, and village priests who come to town to inform, or are returning home when the information has been lodged. Rooms in the 'Serbia' are also occupied by couples from the town for the night or a few days.

Spring. About three in the afternoon. The curtains of the open windows stir gently, and the room smells of kerosene and baked cabbage. It is the landlady warming up on her stove a *bigoss à la Polonaise* of cabbage, pork fat, and sausage, with a great deal of pepper and bay leaves. She is a widow between thirty-six and forty, a strong, quick, good-looking woman. The hair that she wears in curls over her forehead has a strong tinge of grey; but her face is fresh, her big sensual mouth red, and her young dark eyes moist and playfully sly. Her name is Anna Friedrichovna. She is half German, half Pole, and comes from the Baltic Provinces; but her close friends call her Friedrich simply, which suits her determined character better. She is quick-tempered, scolds and talks bawdy. Sometimes she fights with her porters and the lodgers who have been on the spree; she drinks as well as any man, and has a mad passion for dancing. She changes from abuse to laughing in a second. She has but small respect for the law, receives lodgers without passports, and with her own hands, as she says, 'chucks into the street' those who don't pay up—that is, she unlocks his door while he is out, and puts all his things in the passage or on the stairs, and sometimes in her own room. The police are friendly with her for her hospitality, her cheerful character, and particularly for the gay, easy, unceremonious, disinterested complaisance with which she responds to man's passing emotions.

She has four children. The two eldest, Romka and Alychka, have not yet come back from school, and the younger, Adka, seven, and Edka, five, strong brats with cheeks mottled with mud, blotches, tear-stains, and the sunburn of early spring, are always to be found near their mother. Both of them hold on to the table leg and beg. They are perpetually hungry, because their mother does not pay much attention to food; they eat anyhow, at different times, sending into a little general shop for anything they want. Sticking out his lips in a circle, frowning, and looking out under his forehead, Adka roars in a loud bass: 'That 's what you 're like. You won't give me a taste.' 'Let me try,' Edka speaks through his nose, scratching his calf with his bare foot.

At the table by the window sits Lieutenant Valerian Ivanovich Tchijhevich of the Army Reserve. Before him is the register, in which he enters the lodgers' passports. But after yesterday's affair the work goes badly; the letters wave about and crawl away. His trembling fingers quarrel with the pen. There is a roaring in his ears like the telegraph poles in autumn. At times it seems to him that his head is beginning to swell, to swell . . . and the table, the book, the inkstand, and the lieutenant's hand go terribly far away and become quite tiny. Then again the book comes up to his very eyes, the inkstand grows and repeats itself, and his head grows small, turns to queer strange sizes.

Lieutenant Tchijhevich's appearance speaks of former beauty and lost position; his black hair bristles, and a bald patch shows on the nape of his neck. His beard is fashionably trimmed to a sharp point. His face is lean, dirty, pale, dissipated. On it is, as it were written, the full history of the lieutenant's obvious weaknesses and secret diseases.

His situation in the 'Serbia' is complicated. He goes to the magistrates on Anna Friedrichovna's behalf. He hears the children's lessons and teaches them deportment, keeps the house register, makes out the lodgers' accounts, reads the newspaper aloud in the morning and talks of politics. He usually sleeps in one of the vacant rooms and, in case of an influx of guests, in the passage on an ancient sofa, whose springs and stuffing stick out together. When this happens the lieutenant carefully hangs all his property on nails above the sofa: his overcoat, cap, his morning coat, shiny with age and white in the seams but tolerably clean, a 'Monopole' paper collar, an officer's cap with a blue band; but he puts his notebook and his handkerchief with some one else's initials under his pillow.

The widow keeps her lieutenant under her thumb. 'Marry me and I 'll do anything for you,' she promises. 'Full equipment, all the linen you want, a fine pair of boots and goloshes as well. You 'll have everything, and on holidays I 'll let you wear my late husband's watch with the chain.' But the lieutenant is still thinking about it. He values his freedom, and sets high store by his former dignity as an officer. However, he is wearing out some of the older portions of the deceased's linen.

II

From time to time storms break out in the landlady's room. Sometimes it happens that the lieutenant, with the assistance of his pupil Romka, sells a heap of somebody else's books to a second-hand dealer. Sometimes he takes advantage of the landlady's absence to intercept the payment for a room by day. Or he secretly begins to have playful relations with the servant-maid. Just the other day the lieutenant abused Anna Friedrichovna's credit in the public-house over the way. This came to light, and a quarrel raged, with abuse and a fight in the corridor. The doors of all the rooms opened, and men and women poked their heads out in curiosity. Anna Friedrichovna shouted so loud that she was heard in the street :

'You get out of here, you blackguard, get out, you tramp ! I 've spent on you every penny of the money I 've earned by sweating blood. You fill your belly with the farthings I sweat for my children ! '

'You fill your belly with our farthings,' squalled the schoolboy Romka, making faces at him from behind his mother's skirt.

'You fill your belly ! ' Adka and Edka accompanied from a distance.

Arseny the porter, in stony silence, pressed

his chest against the lieutenant. From room No. 9, the valiant possessor of a magnificently parted black beard leaned out to his waist in his underclothes, with a round hat for some reason perched on his head, and resolutely gave his advice :

'Arseny, give him one between the eyes.'

Thus the lieutenant was driven to the stairs ; but there was a broad window opening on to these very stairs from the corridor. Anna Friedrichovna hung out of it and still went on shouting after the lieutenant :

'You dirty beast . . . you murderer . . . scoundrel . . . Kiev gutter-sweeping !'

'Gutter-sweeping !' 'Gutter-sweeping !' the brats in the corridor strained their voices, shouting.

'Don't come eating here any more ! Take your filthy things away with you. Take them. Take them !'

The things the lieutenant had left upstairs in his haste descended on him : a stick, his paper collar, and his notebook. The lieutenant halted on the bottom stair, raised his head, and brandished his fist. His face was pale, a bruise showed red beneath his left eye.

'You just wait, you scum. I tell everything in the proper quarter. Ah ! ah . . . They 're a lot of pimps, robbing the lodgers !'

'You just sling your hook while you 've got a whole skin,' said Arseny sternly, pressing on the lieutenant from behind and pushing him with his shoulder.

'Get away, you swine! You've not the right to lay a finger on an officer,' the lieutenant proudly exclaimed. 'I know about everything! You let people in here without passports! You receive—you receive stolen goods. . . . You keep a broth——'

At this point Arseny seized the lieutenant adroitly from behind. The door slammed with a shattering noise. The two men rolled out into the street together like a ball, and thence came an angry: 'Brothel!'

This morning, as it had always happened before, Lieutenant Tchijhevich came back penitent, with a bouquet of lilac torn out of somebody's garden. His face was weary. A dim blue surrounded his hollow eyes. His forehead was yellow, his clothes unbrushed, and there were feathers in his hair. The reconciliation goes slowly. Anna Friedrichovna hasn't yet had her fill of her lover's submissive look and repentant words. Besides, she is a little jealous of the three nights her Valerian has passed, she knows not where.

'Anna, darling, . . . where . . .' the lieutenant began in an extraordinarily meek and tender falsetto, slightly tremulous even.

'Wha-at! Who 's Anna darling, I 'd like to know,' the landlady contemptuously cut him short. 'I 'm not Anna darling to any scum of a road sweeper!'

'But I only wanted to ask what address I was to write for "Praskovia Uvertiesheva, 34 years old," there 's nothing written down here.'

'Put her down at the Rag-market, and put yourself there, too. You 're a pretty pair. Or put yourself in a doss-house.'

'Dirty beast,' thinks the lieutenant, but he only gives a deep, submissive sigh. 'You 're very nervous to-day, Anna, darling!'

'Nervous! Whatever I am, I know I 'm an honest, hard-working woman. . . . Get out of the way, you bastards,' she shouts at the children, and suddenly, 'Shlop, shlop'—two well-aimed smacks with the spoon come down on Adka's and Edka's foreheads. The boys begin to snivel.

'There 's a curse on my business, and on me,' the landlady growls angrily. 'When I lived with my husband I never had any sorrows. Now, all the porters are drunkards, and all the maids are thieves. Sh! you cursed brats! . . . That Proska . . . she hasn't been here two days when she steals the stockings from the girl in No. 12. Other people go off to pubs with other people's money, and never do a stroke. . . .'

The lieutenant knew perfectly who Anna Friedrichovna was speaking about, but he maintained a concentrated silence. The smell of the *bigoss* inspired him with some faint hopes. Then the door opened and Arseny the porter entered without taking off his hat with the three gold braids. He looks like an Albino eunuch, and his dirty face is pitted. This is at least the fortieth time he has had this place with Anna Friedrichovna. He keeps it until the first fit of drinking, when the landlady herself beats him and puts him into the streets, first having taken away the symbol of his authority, his three-braided cap.

Then Arseny puts a white Caucasian fur hat on his head and a dark blue pince-nez on his nose, and swaggers in the public-house opposite until he 's drunk everything on him away, and at the end of his spree he will cry on the bosom of the indifferent waiter about his hopeless love for Friedrich and threaten to murder Lieutenant Tchijhevich. When he sobers down he comes to the ' Serbia ' and falls at his landlady's feet. And she takes him back again, because the porter who succeeded Arseny had already managed in this short time to steal from her, to get drunk, to make a row and be taken off to the police station.

' You . . . have you come from the steamer ? ' Anna Friedrichovna asked.

' Yes. I 've brought half a dozen pilgrims. It was a job to get 'em away from Jacob—the " Commercial." He was just leading them off, when I comes up to him and says, " It 's all the same to me, I says, go wherever you like. But as there are people who don't know these places, and I 'm very sorry for you, I tell you straight you 'd better not go with that man. In their hotel last week they put some powder in a pilgrim's food and robbed him." So I got them away. Afterwards Jacob shook his fist at me in the distance, and called out : " You just wait, Arseny. I 'll get you. You won't get away from me!" But when that happens, I'll do it myself. . . .'

'All right,' the landlady interrupted. 'I don't care twopence about your Jacob. What price did you fix?'

'Thirty kopeks. I did my best, but I couldn't make them give more.'

'You fool. You can't do anything. . . . Give them No. 2.'

'All in the one room?'

'You fool. Two rooms, each. . . . Of course, all in one room. Bring three mattresses from the old ones, and tell them that they're not to lie on the sofa. These pilgrims have always got bugs. Get along!'

When he had gone the lieutenant said in a tender and solicitous undertone: 'Anna, darling, I wonder why you allow him to enter the room in his hat. It is disrespectful to you, both as a lady and proprietress. And then—consider my position. I'm an officer in Reserve, and he is a private. It's rather awkward.'

But Anna Friedrichovna leapt upon him in fresh exasperation: 'Don't you poke your nose in where it's not wanted. Of-ficer indeed! There are plenty of officers like you spending the night in a shelter. Arseny's a working man. He earns his bread . . . not like . . . Get away, you lazy brats, take your hands away!'

'Ye-es, but give us something to eat,' roars Adka.

'Give us something to eat. . . .'

Meanwhile the *bigoss* is ready. Anna Friedrichovna clatters the dishes on the table. The lieutenant keeps his head busily down over the register. He is completely absorbed in his business.

'Well, sit down,' the landlady abruptly invited him.

'No thanks, Anna, darling. Eat, yourself. I'm not very keen,' Tchijhevich said, without turning round, in a stifled voice, loudly swallowing.

'You do what you are told. . . . He's giving himself airs, too. . . . Come on!'

'Immediately, this very minute. I'll just finish the last page. "The certificate issued by the Bilden Rural District Council . . . of the province . . . number 2039. . . ." Ready.' The lieutenant rose and rubbed his hands. 'I love working.'

'H'm. You call that work,' the landlady snorted in disdain. 'Sit down.'

'Anna, darling, just one . . . little . . .'

'You can manage without.'

But since peace is already almost restored, Anna Friedrichovna takes a small, fat-bodied cut-glass decanter from the cupboard, out of which the deceased's father used to drink. Adka spreads his cabbage all over his plate and teases his brother because he has more. Edka is upset and screams:

'Adka's got more. You gave him——'

Shlop! Edka gets a sounding smack with

the spoon upon his forehead. Immediately Anna Friedrichovna continues the conversation as if nothing had happened:

'Tell us another of your lies. I bet you were with some woman.'

'Anna, darling!' the lieutenant exclaimed reproachfully. Then he stopped eating and pressed his hands—in one of which was a fork with a piece of sausage—to his chest. 'I . . . oh, how little you know me. I'd rather have my head cut off than let such a thing happen. When I went away that time, I felt so bitter, so hard! I just walked in the street, and you can imagine, I was drowned in tears. My God,' I thought, 'and I've let myself insult that woman—the one woman whom I love sacredly, madly. . . .'

'That's a pretty story,' put in the landlady, gratified, but still somewhat suspicious.

'You don't believe me,' the lieutenant replied in a quiet, deep, tragic voice. 'Well, I've deserved it. Every night I came to your window and prayed for you in my soul.' The lieutenant instantly tipped the glass into his mouth, took a bite, and went on with his mouth full and his eyes watering:

'I was thinking that if a fire were to break out suddenly or murderers attack, I would prove to you then. . . . I'd have given my life joyfully. Alas! my life is short without that. My days are numbered. . . .'

Meanwhile the landlady fumbled in her purse.

'Go on!' she replied, coquettishly. 'Adka,

here 's the money. Run to Vasily Vasilich's and get a bottle of beer. But tell him it 's got to be fresh. Quick ! '

Breakfast is finished, the *bigoss* eaten, and the beer all drunk, when Romka, the depraved member of the preparatory class of the gymnasium, appears covered in chalk and ink. Still standing at the door he pouts and looks angrily. Then he flings his satchel down on the floor and begins to howl :

' There ! . . . you 've been and eaten everything without me. I 'm as hungry as a do-og.'

' I 've got some more. But I shan't give you any,' Adka teases him, showing him his plate across the room.

' There ! . . . it 's a dirty trick,' Romka drags out the words. ' Mother, tell Adka——'

' Be *quiet* ! ' Anna Friedrichovna cries in a piercing voice. ' Dawdle till it 's dark, why don't you ? Take twopence. Buy yourself some sausage. That 'll do for you.'

' Ye-es, twopence ! You and Valerian Ivanich eat *bigoss*, and you make me go to school. I 'm just like a do-o-o-g.'

' Get *out* ! ' Anna Friedrichovna shouts in a terrible voice, and Romka precipitately disappears. Still he managed to pick his satchel up from the floor. A thought had suddenly come into his head. He would go and sell his books in the Rag-market. In the doorway he ran into his elder sister Alychka, and seized the opportunity to pinch her arm very hard. Alychka entered grumbling aloud :

'Mamma! tell Romka not to pinch.'

She is a handsome girl of thirteen, beginning to develop early, a swarthy, olive brunette, with beautiful dark eyes, which are not at all childish. Her lips are red, full and shining, and on her upper lip, which is lightly covered with a fine black down, there are two delightful moles. She is a general favourite in the house. The men give her chocolates, often invite her into their rooms, kiss her and say impudent things to her. She knows as much as any grown-up, but in these cases she never blushes, but just casts down her long black eyelashes which throw a blue shade on her amber cheeks, and smiles with a strange, modest, tender yet voluptuous, and somehow expectant smile. Her best friend is the woman Eugenia who lives in No. 12—a quiet girl, punctual in paying for her room, a stout blonde, who is kept by a timber merchant, but on her free days invites her cavaliers from the street. Anna Friedrichovna holds her in high esteem, and says of her: 'Well, what does it matter if Eugenia is not quite respectable, she 's an independent woman anyhow.'

Seeing that breakfast is over Alychka gives one of her constrained smiles and says aloud in her thin voice, rather theatrically: 'Ah! you 've finished already. I 'm too late. Mamma! may I go to Eugenia Nicolaievna?'

'Go wherever you like!'

'*Merci!*'

She goes away. After breakfast complete

peace reigns. The lieutenant whispers the most ardent words into the widow's ear, and presses her generous knee under the table. Flushing with the food and beer, she presses her shoulder close to him, then pushes him away and sighs with nervous laughter.

'Yes, Valerian. You 're shameless. The children!'

Adka and Edka look at them, with their fingers in their mouths and their eyes wide open. Their mother suddenly springs upon them.

'Go for a run, you ruffians. Sitting there like dummies in a museum. Quick march!'

'But I don't want to,' roars Adka.

'I don' wan'——'

'I 'll teach you "Don't want to." A halfpenny for candy, and out you go.'

She locks the door after them, sits on the lieutenant's knee, and they begin to kiss.

'You 're not cross, my treasure?' the lieutenant whispers in her ear.

But there is a knock at the door. They have to open. The new chambermaid enters, a tall, gloomy woman with one eye, and says hoarsely, with a ferocious look:

'No. 12 wants a samovar, some tea, and some sugar.'

Anna Friedrichovna impatiently gives out what is wanted. The lieutenant says languidly, stretched on the sofa:

'I would like to rest a bit, Anna, dear. Isn't there a room empty? People are always knocking about here.'

There is only one room empty, No. 5, and

there they go. Their room is long, narrow, and dark, like a skittle-alley, with one window. A bed, a chest of drawers, a blistered brown washstand, and a commode are all its furniture. The landlady and the lieutenant once more begin to kiss ; and they moan like doves on the roof in springtime.

'Anna, darling, if you love me, send for a packet of ten "Cigarettes Plaisir," six kopeks,' says the lieutenant coaxingly, while he undresses.

'Later——'

The spring evening darkens quickly, and it is already night. Through the window comes the whistling of the steamers on the Dnieper, and with it creeps a faint smell of hay, dust, lilac and warm stone. The water falls into the wash-stand, dripping regularly. There is another knock.

'Who 's there ? What the devil are you prowling about for ?' cries Anna Friedrichovna awakened. She jumps barefoot from the bed and angrily opens the door. 'Well, what do you want ?'

Lieutenant Tchijhevich modestly pulls the blanket over his head.

'A student wants a room,' Arseny says behind the door in a stage whisper.

'What student ? Tell him there 's only one room, and that 's two roubles. Is he alone, or with a woman ?'

'Alone.'

'Tell him then: passport and money in advance. I know these students.'

The lieutenant dressed hurriedly. From habit he takes ten seconds over his toilette. Anna Friedrichovna tidies the bed quickly and cleverly. Arseny returns.

'He 's paid in advance,' he said gloomily. 'And here 's the passport.'

The landlady went out into the corridor. Her hair was dishevelled and a fringe was sticking to her forehead. The folds of the pillow were imprinted on her crimson cheeks. Her eyes were unnaturally brilliant. The lieutenant, under cover of her back, slipped into the landlady's room as noiseless as a shadow.

The student was waiting by the window on the stairs. He was already no longer a young man. He was thin and fair-haired, and his face was long and pale, tender and sickly. His good-natured, short-sighted blue eyes, with the faintest shade of a squint, look out as through a mist. He bowed politely to the landlady, at which she smiled in confusion and fastened the top hook of her blouse.

'I should like a room,' he said softly, as if his courage was ebbing. 'I have to go on from here. But I should be obliged for a candle and pen and ink.'

He was shown the skittle-alley.

'Excellent,' he said. 'I couldn't want anything better. It 's wonderful here. Just let me have a pen and ink, please.' He did not require tea or bed-linen.

III

THE lamp was burning in the landlady's room. Alychka sat Turkish fashion in the open window, watching the dark heavy mass of water, lit by electric lamps, wavering below, and the gentle motion of the scant dead green of the poplars along the quay. Two round spots of bright red were burning in her cheeks, and there was a moist and weary light in her eyes. In the cooling air the petulant sound of a valse graciously floated from far away on the other side of the river, where the lights of the café chantant were shining.

They were drinking tea with shop bought raspberry jam. Adka and Edka crumbled pieces of black bread into their saucers, and made a kind of porridge. They smeared their faces, foreheads, and noses with it. They blew bubbles in their saucers. Romka, returned with a black eye, was hastily taking noisy sups of tea from a saucer. Lieutenant Tchijhevich had unbuttoned his waistcoat, extruding his paper dickey, and half lay on the sofa, perfectly happy in this domestic idyll.

'Thank God, all the rooms are taken,' Anna Friedrichovna sighed dreamily.

'You see, it's all due to my lucky touch,' said the lieutenant. 'When I came back, everything began to look up.'

'There, tell us another.'

'No, really, my touch is amazingly lucky. By God, it is! In the regiment, when Captain Gorojhevsky took the bank, he always used to make me sit beside him. My God! how those men used to play! That same Gorojhevsky, when he was still a subaltern, at the time of the Turkish War, won twelve thousand. Our regiment came to Bukarest. Of course, the officers had pots of money—nothing to do with it—no women. They began cards. Suddenly, Gorojhevsky pounced on a sharp. You could see he was a crook by the cut of his lug. But he faked the cards so cleverly that you couldn't possibly get hold of him. . . .'

'Wait a second. I'll be back in a moment,' interrupted the landlady. 'I only want to give out a towel.'

She went out. The lieutenant stealthily came near to Alychka and bent close to her. Her beautiful profile, dark against the background of night, took on a subtle, tender outline of silver in the radiance of the electric lamps.

'What are you thinking about, Alychka—perhaps I should say, whom?' he asked in a sweet tremolo.

She turned away from him. But he quickly lifted the thick plait of her hair and kissed her beneath her hair on her warm thin neck, greedily smelling the perfume of her skin.

'I'll tell mother,' whispered Alychka, without drawing away.

The door opened. It was Anna Friedrichovna

returned. Immediately the lieutenant began to talk, unnaturally loud and free.

'Really, it would be wonderful to be on a boat with your beloved or your dearest friend on a spring night like this. . . . Well, to continue, Anna, darling. So Gorojhevsky dropped a cool six thousand, if you 'll believe me! At last some one gave him a word of advice. He said: "*Basta*—I 'm not having any more of this. You won't mind if we put a nail through the pack to the table and tear off our cards?" The fellow wanted to get out of it. Gorojhevsky took out his revolver: "You 'll play, you dog, or I 'll blow a hole in your head!" There was nothing for it. The crook sat down, so flustered that he clean forgot there was a mirror behind him. Gorojhevsky could see every one of his cards. So Gorojhevsky not only got his own back, but raked in a clear eleven thousand into the bargain. He even had the nail mounted in gold, and he wears it as a charm on his watch chain.'

IV

At the moment the student was sitting on the bed in No. 5. On the commode before him stood a candle and a sheet of writing paper. The student was writing quickly; then he stopped for a moment, whispered to himself, shook his head, smiled a constrained smile and wrote again. He had just dipped his pen deep in the ink. He spooned up the liquid wax round the wick with it and poked the mixture into the flame. It crackled and splashed about everywhere with little blue darting flames. The firework reminded the student of something funny, dimly remembered from his distant childhood. He looked at the flame of the candle, his eyes narrowed, and a sad, distracted smile formed upon his lips. Then suddenly as though awakened he shook his head, sighed, wiped his pen on the sleeve of his blue blouse, and continued to write:

'Tell them everything in my letter, which you will believe, I know. They will not understand me all the same; but you will have simple words that will be intelligible to them. One thing is very strange. Here am I writing to you, yet I know that in ten or fifteen minutes I shall shoot myself—and the thought does not frighten me at all. But when that huge grey colonel of the gendarmes went red all over and stamped his feet and swore, I was quite lost. When he cried that my obstinacy was useless, and only ruined my comrades and myself, that Bieloussov as well as Knigge and Soloveitchik had confessed, I confessed too. I, who am not afraid of death, was afraid of the shouting of this dull, narrow-minded clod, petrified with professional conceit. What is more disgusting still, he dared not shout at the others. He was courteous, obliging, and sugary to them, like a suburban dentist. He was even a Liberal. But in me he saw at once a weak, yielding will. You can feel it in people at a mere glance—there 's no need of words.

'Yes, I confess that it was all mad and contemptible and ridiculous and loathsome. But it could not be otherwise. And if it were to be again, it would happen as before. Desperately brave generals are often frightened of mice. Sometimes they even boast of their little weakness. But I say with sorrow that I fear these wooden people, whose view of the world is rigid and unchangeable, who are stupidly self-confident, and have no hesitations, worse than death. If you knew how timid and uncomfortable I am before huge policemen, ugly Petersburg porters, typists in the editorial offices of magazines, magistrates' clerks, and snarling stationmasters! Once I had to have my signature witnessed at the police station, and the mere look of the fat inspector, with his ginger moustache as big as a palm tree, his important chest and his fish eyes, who interrupted me continually, would not hear me out, forgot me altogether for minutes on end, or suddenly pretended that he could not understand the simplest Russian words—his mere look made me so disgustingly frightened that I could catch an insinuating, servile inflection in my voice.

'Who's to blame for it? I'll tell you. My mother. She was the original cause of the fouling and corruption of my soul with a vile cowardice. She became a widow when she was still young, and my first impressions as a child are indissolubly mixed up with wandering in other people's houses, servile smiles, petty intolerable insults, complaisance, lying, whining pitiful grimaces, the vile phrases: "a little drop, a little bit, a little cup of tea." . . . I was made to kiss my benefactors' hands—men and women. My mother protested that I did not like this dainty or that; she lied that I had a weak stomach, because she knew that the children of the house would have more, and the host would like it. The servants sneered at us on the sly. They called me hunchback, because I had a stoop from childhood. They called my mother a hanger-on and a beggar in my presence. And to make the kind people laugh my mother herself would put her shabby old leather cigarette case to her nose and bend it double: "That's my darling Levoushka's nose." They laughed, and I blushed and suffered endlessly for her and for myself; but I kept silent, because I must not speak in the presence of my benefactors. I hated them, for looking at me as though I were a stone, idly and lazily thrusting their hand to my mouth for me to kiss. I hated and feared them, as I still hate and fear all decided, self-satisfied, rigid, sober people, who know everything beforehand—club orators; old red-faced hairy professors, who flirt with their harmless Liberalism; imposing, anointed canons of cathedrals; colonels of the gendarmerie; radical lady-doctors, who everlastingly repeat bits out of manifestoes, whose soul is as cold, as cruel, and as flat as a marble table-top. When I speak to them I feel that there is on my face a loathsome mark, a servile officious smile that is not mine, and I despise myself for my thin wheedling voice, in which I can catch the echo of my mother's note. These people's souls are dead: their thoughts are fixed in straight inflexible lines; and they are merciless as only a convinced and stupid man can be.

'I spent the years between seven and ten in a state charity school on the Froebel system. The mistresses were all soured old maids, all suffering from inflammations, and they instilled into us respect for the generous authorities, taught us how to spy on each other and tell tales, how to envy the favourites, and, most important of all, how to behave as quietly as possible. But we boys educated ourselves in thieving and abuses. Later on—still charity—I was taken as a state boarder into a gymnasium. The inspectors visited and spied on us. We learnt like parrots: smoking in the third form; drinking in the fourth; in the fifth, the first prostitute and the first vile disease.

'Then suddenly there arose new, young words like a wind, impetuous dreams, free, fiery, thoughts. My mind opened eagerly to meet them, but my soul was already ruined for ever, soiled and dead. It had been bitten by a mean, weak-nerved timidity, like a tick in a dog's ear: you tear it off, but the small head remains to grow again into a complete, loathsome insect.

'I was not the only one to die of the moral contagion, though perhaps I was the weakest of all. But all the past generation has grown up in an atmosphere of sanctimonious tranquillity, of forced respect to its elders, of lack of all individuality and dumbness. A curse on this vile age, of silence and poverty, this peaceful prosperous life under the dumb shadow of pious reaction: for the quiet degradation of the human soul is more horrible than all the barricades and slaughter in the world.

'Strange that when I am alone with my own will, I am not only no coward, but there are few people I know who are more ready to risk their lives. I have walked from one window-sill to another five stories above ground and looked down below; I 've swum so far out into the sea that my hands and feet would move no more, and I had to lie on my back and rest to avoid cramp. And many things besides. Finally, in ten minutes I shall kill myself—and that is something. But I am afraid of people. I fear people! When from my room I hear drunken men swearing and fighting in the street I go pale with terror. When I imagine at night as I lie in bed, an empty square with a squadron of Cossacks galloping in with a roar, my heart stops beating, my body grows cold all over, and my fingers contract convulsively. I am always frightened of something which exists in the majority of people, but which I cannot explain. The young generation of the period of transition were like me. In our mind we despised our slavery, but we ourselves became cowardly slaves. Our hatred was deep and passionate, but barren, like the mad love of a eunuch.

'But you will understand everything, and explain it all to the comrades to whom I say before I die, that in spite of all, I love and respect them. Perhaps they will believe you when you tell them that I did not die wholly because I had betrayed them vilely and against my will. I know that there is in the world nothing more horrible than the horrible word "Traitor." It moves from lips to ears, from lips to ears, and kills a man alive. Oh, I could set right my mistake were I not born and bred a slave of human impudence, cowardice, and stupidity. But because I am this slave, I die. In these great fiery days it is disgraceful, difficult, no, quite impossible for men like me to live.

'Yes, my darling, I have heard, seen, and read much in the last year. I tell you there came a moment of awful volcanic eruption. The flame of long pent-up anger broke out and overwhelmed everything: fear of the morrow, respect for parents, love of life, peaceful joys of family happiness. I know of boys, hardly more than children, who refused to have a bandage on their eyes when they were executed. I myself saw people who underwent tortures, yet uttered not a word. It was all born suddenly, in a tempestuous wind. Eagles awoke out of turkey eggs. Let who will arrest their flight!

'I am quite certain that a sixth-form boy of to-day would proclaim the demands of his party, firmly, intelligently, perhaps with a touch of arrogance, in the presence of all the crowned heads and all the chiefs of police in Europe, in any throne room. It is true the precious schoolboy is very nearly ridiculous, but a sacred respect for his proud free self is already growing up within him, a respect for everything that has been corroded in us by spiritual poverty and anxious paternal morality. We must go to the devil.

'It is just eight minutes to nine. At nine exactly it will be all over with me. A dog barks outside—one, two—then is silent for a little and—one, two, three. Perhaps, when my consciousness has been put out, and with it everything has disappeared from me for ever: towns, public squares, hooting steamers, mornings and nights, apartment rooms, ticking clocks, people, animals, the air, the light and dark, time and space, and there is nothing—then there will be no thought of this "nothing"! Perhaps the dog will go on barking for a long while to-night, first twice, then three times. . . .

'Five minutes to nine. A funny idea is occupying me. I think that a human thought is like a current from some electric centre, an intense, radiating vibration of the imponderable ether, poured out in the spaces of the world, and passing with equal ease through the atoms of stone, iron, and air. A thought springs from my brain and all the sphere of the universe begins to tremble, to ripple round me like water into which a stone is flung, like a sound about a vibrating string. And I think that when a man passes away his consciousness is put out, but his thought still remains, trembling in its former place. Perhaps the thoughts and dreams of all the people who were before me in this long, gloomy room are still hovering round me, directing my will in secret; and perhaps to-morrow a casual tenant of this room will suddenly begin to think of life, of death, and suicide, because I leave my thoughts behind me here. And who can say whether my thoughts, independent of weight and time and the obstacles of matter, are not at the same moment being caught by mysterious, delicate, but unconscious receivers in the brain of an inhabitant of Mars as well as in the brain of the dog who barks outside? Ah, I think that nothing in the world vanishes utterly—nothing—not only what is said, but what is thought. All our deeds and words and thoughts are little streams, trickling springs underground. I believe, I see, they meet, flow together into river-heads, ooze to the surface, run into rivulets, and now they rush in the wild, broad stream of the harmonious River of Life. The River of Life—how great it is! Sooner or later it will bear everything away, and wash down all the strongholds which imprisoned the freedom of the spirit. Where a shoal of triviality was before, there will be the profoundest depth of heroism. In a moment it will bear me away to a cold, remote, and inconceivable land, and perhaps within a year it will pour in torrents over all this mighty town and flood it and carry away in its waters not merely its ruins, but its very name.

'Perhaps what I am writing is all ridiculous. I have two minutes left. The candle is burning and the clock ticking hurriedly in front of me. The dog is still barking. What if there remain nothing of me—nothing of me, or in me, but one thing only, the last sensation, perhaps pain, perhaps the sound of the pistol, perhaps wild naked terror; but it will remain for ever, for thousands of millions of centuries, in the millionth degree.

'The hand has reached the hour. We 'll know it all now. No, wait. Some ridiculous modesty made me get up and lock the door. Good-bye. One word more. Surely the obscure soul of the dog must be far more susceptible to the vibrations of thought than the human. . . . Do they not bark because they feel the presence of a dead man? This dog that barks downstairs too. But in a second, new monstrous currents will rush out of the central battery of my brain and touch the poor brain of the dog. It will begin to howl with a queer, intolerable terror. . . . Good-bye, I 'm going!'

The student sealed the letter—for some reason he carefully closed the ink-pot with a cork—and took a Browning out of his jacket pocket. He turned the safety catch from *sur* to *feu*. He put his legs apart so that he could stand firm, and closed his eyes. Suddenly, with both hands he swiftly raised the revolver to his right temple and pulled the trigger.

'What 's that ?' Anna Friedrichovna asked in alarm.

'That 's your student shooting himself,' the lieutenant said carelessly. 'They 're such *canaille*—these students. . . .'

But Anna Friedrichovna jumped up and ran into the corridor, the lieutenant following at his leisure. From room No. 5 came a sour smell of gas and smokeless powder. They looked through the keyhole. The student lay on the floor.

Within five minutes there was a thick, black, eager crowd standing in the street outside the hotel. In exasperation Arseny drove the outsiders away from the stairs. Commotion was everywhere in the hotel. A locksmith broke open the door of the room. The caretaker ran for the police ; the chambermaid for the doctor. After some time appeared the police inspector, a tall thin young man with white hair, white eyelashes, and a white moustache. He was in uniform. His wide trousers were so full that they fell half way down over his polished jack-boots. Immediately he pressed his way through the public, and roared with the voice of authority, sticking out his bright eyes :

'Get back ! Clear off ! I can't understand what it is you find so curious here. Nothing at all. You, sir ! . . . I ask you once more. And he looks like an intellectual, in a bowler hat. . . . What 's that ? I 'll show you "police tyranny." Mikhailtchuk, just take note of that man ! Hi, where are you crawling to, boy ? I 'll——'

The door was broken open. Into the room

burst Anna Friedrichovna, the police inspector, the lieutenant, the four children ; for witnesses, one policeman and two caretakers ; and after them, the doctor. The student lay on the floor, with his face buried in the strip of grey carpet by the bed. His left arm was bent beneath his chest, his right flung out. The pistol lay on one side. Under his head was a pool of dark blood, and a little round hole in his left temple. The candle was still burning, and the clock on the commode ticked hurriedly.

A short procès-verbal was composed in wooden official terms, and the suicide's letter attached to it. . . . The two caretakers and the policeman carried the corpse downstairs. Arseny lighted the way, lifting the lamp above his head. Anna Friedrichovna, the police inspector and the lieutenant looked on through the window in the corridor upstairs. The bearers' movements got out of step at the turning ; they jammed between the wall and the banisters, and the one who was supporting the head from behind let go his hands. The head knocked sharply against the stairs—one, two, three. . . .

'Serves him right, serves him right,' angrily cried the landlady from the window. 'Serves him right, the scoundrel ! I 'll give you a good tip for that ! '

'You 're very bloodthirsty, Madame Siegmayer,' the police inspector remarked playfully, twisting his moustache, and looking sideways at the end of it.

'Why, he 'll get me into the papers, now. I 'm a poor working woman ; and now, all along of him, people will keep away from my hotel.'

'Naturally,' the inspector kindly agreed. 'I can't understand these student fellows. They don't want to study. They brandish a red flag, and then shoot themselves. They don't want to understand what their parents must feel. They 're bought by Jewish money, damn them! But there are decent men at the same game, sons of noblemen, priests, merchants. . . . A nice lot! However, I give you my compliments. . . .'

'No, no, no, no! Not for anything in the world!' The landlady pulled herself together. 'We 'll have supper in a moment. A nice little bit of herring. Otherwise, I won't let you go, for anything.'

'To tell the truth——' The inspector spoke in perplexity. 'Very well. As a matter of fact, I was going to drop in to Nagourno's opposite for something. Our work,' he said, politely making way for the landlady through the door, 'is hard. Sometimes we don't get a bite all day long.'

All three had a good deal of vodka at supper. Anna Friedrichovna, red all over, with shining eyes and lips like blood, slipped off one of her shoes beneath the table and pressed the inspector's foot. The lieutenant frowned, became jealous, and all the while tried to begin a story of 'In the regiment——' The inspector did not listen, but interrupted with terrific tales of 'In the police——' Each tried to be as contemptuous of and inattentive to the other as he could. They were both like a couple of young dogs that have just met in the yard.

'You 're everlastingly talking of "In the regiment,"' said the inspector, looking not at the lieutenant, but the landlady. 'Would you mind my asking what was the reason why you left the service?'

'Well, . . .' the lieutenant replied, offended. 'Would you like me to ask you how you came to be in the police; how you came to such a life?'

Here Anna Friedrichovna brought the 'Monopan' musical box out of the corner and made Tchijhevich turn the handle. After some invitation the inspector danced a polka with her—she jumped about like a little girl, and the curls on her forehead jumped with her. Then the inspector turned the handle while the lieutenant danced, pressing the landlady's arm to his left side, with his head flung back. Alychka also danced with downcast eyes, and her tender dissipated smile on her lips. The inspector was saying his last good-bye, when Romka appeared.

'There, I 've been seeing the student off, and while I was away you 've been—— I 'm treated like a do-o-og.'

And what was once a student now lay in the cold cellar of an anatomical theatre, in a zinc box, standing on ice—lit by a yellow gas flame, yellow and repulsive. On his bare right leg above the knee in gross ink figures was written '14.' That was his number in the anatomical theatre.

II

CAPTAIN RIBNIKOV

CAPTAIN RIBNIKOV

I

ON the very day when the awful disaster to the Russian fleet at Tsushima was nearing its end, and the first vague and alarming reports of that bloody triumph of the Japanese were being circulated over Europe, Staff-Captain Ribnikov, who lived in an obscure alley in the Pieski quarter, received the following telegram from Irkutsk: *Send lists immediately watch patient pay debts.*

Staff-Captain Ribnikov immediately informed his landlady that he was called away from Petersburg on business for a day or two, and told her not to worry about his absence. Then he dressed himself, left the house, and never returned to it again.

Only five days had passed when the landlady was summoned to the police station to give evidence about her missing lodger. She was a tall woman of forty-five, the honest widow of an ecclesiastical official, and in a simple and straightforward manner she told all that she knew of him. Her lodger was a quiet, poor, simple man, a moderate eater, and polite. He neither drank nor smoked, rarely went out of the house, and had no visitors. She could say nothing more, in spite of all her respectful terror of the inspector of gendarmerie, who moved his luxurious moustaches in a terrifying way and had a fine stock of abuse on hand.

During this five days' interval Staff-Captain Ribnikov ran or drove over the whole of Petersburg. Everywhere, in the streets, restaurants, theatres, tramcars, the railway stations, this dark lame little officer appeared. He was strangely talkative, untidy, not particularly sober, dressed in an infantry uniform, with an all-over red collar—a perfect type of the rat attached to military hospitals, or the commissariat, or the War Office. He also appeared more than once at the Staff Office, the Committee for the Care of the Wounded, at police stations, at the office of the Military Governor, at the Cossack headquarters, and at dozens of other offices, irritating the officials by his senseless grumbling and complaints, by his abject begging, his typical infantry rudeness, and his noisy patriotism. Already every one knew by heart that he had served in the Army Transport, had been wounded in the head at Liao-Yang, and touched in the leg in the retreat from Mukden. 'Why the devil hasn't he received a gratuity before now! Why haven't they given him his daily money and his travelling expenses! And his last two months pay! He is absolutely ready to give his last drop of blood—damn it all—for the Czar, the throne, and the country, and he will return to the Far East the moment his leg has healed. But the cursed leg won't heal—a hundred devils take it. Imagine only—gangrene! Look yourself——' and he put his wounded leg on a chair, and was already eagerly pulling up his trouser; but he was stopped every time by a squeamish and compassionate shyness. His bustling and nervous familiarity, his startled, frightened look, which bordered strangely on impertinence, his stupidity, his persistent and frivolous curiosity taxed to the utmost the patience of men occupied in important and terribly responsible scribbling.

In vain it was explained to him in the kindest possible way that he had come to the wrong place; that he ought to apply at such and such a place; that he must produce certain papers; that they will let him know the result. He understood nothing, absolutely nothing. But it was impossible to be very angry with him; he was so helpless, so easily scared and simple, and if any one lost patience and interrupted him, he only smiled and showed his gums with a foolish look, bowed hastily again and again, and rubbed his hands in confusion. Or he would suddenly say in a hoarse, ingratiating tone:

'Couldn't you give me one small smoke? I'm dying to smoke. And I haven't a cent to buy them. "Blessed are the poor.... Poverty's no crime," as they say—but sheer indecency.'

With that he disarmed the most disagreeable and dour officials. He was given a cigarette, and allowed to sit by the extreme corner of the table. Unwillingly, and of course in an off-hand way, they would answer his importunate questions about what was happening at the war. But there was something very affecting and childishly sincere in the sickly curiosity with which this unfortunate, grubby, impoverished wounded officer of the line followed the war. Quite simply, out of mere humanity, they wanted to reassure, to inform, and encourage him; and therefore they spoke to him more frankly than to the rest.

His interest in everything which concerned Russo-Japanese events was so deep that while they were making some complicated inquiry for him he would wander from room to room, and table to table, and the moment he caught a couple of words about the war he would approach and listen with his habitual strained and silly smile.

When he finally went away, as well as a sense of relief he would leave a vague, heavy and disquieting regret behind him. Often well-groomed, dandified staff-officers referred to him with dignified acerbity:

'And that's a Russian officer! Look at that *type*. Well, it's pretty plain why we're losing battle after battle. Stupid, dull, without the least sense of his own dignity—poor old Russia!'

During these busy days Captain Ribnikov took a room in a dirty little hotel near the railway station.

Though he had with him a Reserve officer's proper passport, for some reason he found it necessary to declare that his papers were at present in the Military Governor's office. Into the hotel he took his things, a hold-all containing a rug and pillow, a travelling bag, and a cheap, new box, with some underclothing and a complete outfit of mufti.

Subsequently, the servants gave evidence that he used to come to the hotel late and as if a little the worse for drink, but always regularly gave the door porter twopence for a tip. He never used to sleep more than three or four hours, sometimes without undressing. He used to get up early and pace the room for hours. In the afternoon he would go off.

From time to time he sent telegrams to Irkutsk from various post offices, and all the telegrams expressed a deep concern for some one wounded and seriously ill, probably a person very dear to the captain's heart.

It was with this same curious busy, uncouth man that Vladimir Ivanovich Schavinsky, a journalist on a large Petersburg paper, once met.

II

JUST before he went off to the races, Schavinsky dropped into the dingy little restaurant called 'The Glory of Petrograd,' where the reporters used to gather at two in the afternoon to exchange thoughts and information. The company was rough and ready, gay, cynical, omniscient, and hungry enough; and Schavinsky, who was to some degree an aristocrat of the newspaper world, naturally did not belong to it. His bright and amusing Sunday articles, which were not too deep, had a considerable success with the public. He made a great deal of money, dressed well, and had plenty of friends. But he was welcome at 'The Glory of Petrograd' as well, on account of his free sharp tongue and the affable generosity with which he lent his fellow-writers half sovereigns. On this day the reporters had promised to procure a race-card for him, with mysterious annotations from the stable.

Vassily, the porter, took off Schavinsky's overcoat, with a friendly and respectful smile.

'If you please, Vladimir Ivanovitch, company 's all there. In the big saloon, where Prokhov waits.'

And Prokhov, stout, close-cropped, and red-moustached, also gave him a kindly and familiar smile, as usual not looking straight into the eyes of a respectable customer, but over his head.

'A long time since you've honoured us, Vladimir Ivanovich! This way, please. Everybody's here.'

As usual his fellow-writers sat round the long table hurriedly dipping their pens in the single inkpot and scribbling quickly on long slips of paper. At the same time, without interrupting their labours, they managed to swallow pies, fried sausages and mashed potatoes, vodka and beer, to smoke and exchange the latest news of the town and newspaper gossip that cannot be printed. Some one was sleeping like a log on the sofa with his face in a handkerchief. The air in the saloon was blue, thick and streaked with tobacco smoke.

As he greeted the reporters, Schavinsky noticed the captain, in his ordinary army uniform, among them. He was sitting with his legs apart, resting his hands and chin upon the hilt of a large sword. Schavinsky was not surprised at seeing him, as he had learned not to be surprised at anything in the reporting world. He had often seen lost for weeks in that reckless noisy company,—landowners from the provinces, jewellers, musicians, dancing-masters, actors, circus proprietors, fishmongers, café-chantant managers, gamblers from the clubs, and other members of the most unexpected professions.

When the officer's turn came, he rose, straightened his shoulders, stuck out his elbows, and introduced himself in the proper hoarse, drink-sodden voice of an officer of the line:

'H'm! . . . Captain Ribnikov. . . . Pleased to meet you. . . . You 're a writer too? . . . Delighted. . . . I respect the writing fraternity. The press is the sixth great power. Eh, what?'

With that he grinned, clicked his heels together, shook Schavinsky's hand violently, bowing all the while in a particularly funny way, bending and straightening his body quickly.

'Where have I seen him before?' the uneasy thought flashed across Schavinsky's mind. 'He 's wonderfully like some one. Who can it be?'

Here in the saloon were all the celebrities of the Petersburg reporting world. The Three Musketeers—Kodlubtzov, Riazhkin, and Popov—were never seen except in company. Even their names were so easily pronounced together that they made an iambic tetrameter. This did not prevent them from eternally quarrelling, and from inventing stories of incredible extortion, criminal forgery, slander, and blackmail about each other. There was present also Sergey Kondrashov, whose unrestrained voluptuousness had gained him the name of 'A Pathological Case, not a man.' There was also a man whose name had been effaced by time, like one side of a worn coin, to whom remained only the general nickname 'Matanya,' by which all Petersburg knew him. Concerning the dour-looking Svischov, who wrote paragraphs 'In the police courts,' they said jokingly: 'Svischov is an awful blackmailer—never takes less than three roubles.' The man asleep on the sofa was the long-haired poet Piestrukhin, who supported his fragile, drunken existence by writing lyrics in honour of the imperial birthdays and the twelve Church holidays. There were others besides of no less celebrity, experts in municipal affairs, fires, inquests, in the opening and closing of public gardens.

Said lanky, shock-headed, pimply Matanya: 'They 'll bring you the card immediately, Vladimir Ivanovich. Meanwhile, I commend our brave captain to your attention. He has just returned from the Far East, where, I may say, he made mince-meat of the yellow-faced, squinting, wily enemy. . . . Now, General, fire away!'

The officer cleared his throat and spat sideways on the floor.

'Swine!' thought Schavinsky, frowning.

'My dear chap, the Russian soldier 's not to be sneezed at!' Ribnikov bawled hoarsely, rattling his sword. '"Epic heroes!" as the immortal Suvorov said. Eh, what? In a word, . . . but I tell you frankly, our commanders in the East are absolutely worthless! You know the proverb: "Like master, like man." Eh, what? They thieve, play cards, have mistresses . . . and every one knows, where the devil can't manage himself he sends a woman.'

'You were talking about plans, General,' Matanya reminded him.

'Ah! Plans! *Merci!* . . . My head. . . . I've been on the booze all day.' Ribnikov threw a quick, sharp glance at Schavinsky. 'Yes, I was just saying. . . . They ordered a certain colonel of the general staff to make a reconnaissance, and he takes with him a squadron of Cossacks—dare-devils. Hell take 'em! . . . Eh, what? He sets off with an interpreter. Arrives at a village, "What's the name?" The interpreter says nothing. "At him, boys!" The Cossacks instantly use their whips. The interpreter says: "Butundu!" And "Butundu" is Chinese for "I don't understand." Ha-ha! He's opened his mouth—the son of a bitch! The colonel writes down "village, Butundu." They go further to another village. "What's the name?" "Butundu." "What! Butundu again?" "Butundu." Again the colonel enters it "village, Butundu." So he entered ten villages under the name of "Butundu," and turned into one of Tchekov's types—"Though you are Ivanov the seventh," says he, "you're a fool all the same."'

'Oh, you know Tchekov?' asked Schavinsky.

'Who? Tchekov? old Anton? You bet—damn him. . . . We're friends—we're often drunk together. . . . "Though you are the seventh," says he, "you're a fool all the same."'

'Did you meet him in the East?' asked Schavinsky quickly.

'Yes, exactly, in the East, Tchekov and I, old man. . . . "Though you are the seventh——"'

While he spoke Schavinsky observed him closely. Everything in him agreed with the conventional army type: his voice, manner, shabby uniform, his coarse and threadbare speech. Schavinsky had had the chance of observing hundreds of such debauched captains. They had the same grin, the samc 'Hell take 'em,' twisted their moustaches to the left and right with the same bravado; they hunched their shoulders, stuck out their elbows, rested picturesquely on their sword and clanked imaginary spurs. But there was something individual about him as well, something different, as it were, locked away, which Schavinsky had never seen, neither could he define it—some intense, inner, nervous force. The impression he had was this: Schavinsky would not have been at all surprised if this croaking and drunken soldier of fortune had suddenly begun to talk of subtle and intellectual matters, with ease and illumination, elegantly; neither would he have been surprised at some mad, sudden, frenzied, even bloody prank on the captain's part.

What struck Schavinsky chiefly in the captain's looks was the different impression he made full face and in profile. Side face, he was a common Russian, faintly Kalmuck, with a small, protruding forehead under a pointed skull, a formless Russian nose, shaped like a plum, thin stiff black moustache and sparse beard, the grizzled hair cropped close, with a complexion burnt to a dark yellow by the sun. . . . But when he turned full face Schavinsky was immediately reminded of some one. There was something extraordinarily familiar about him, but this ' something ' was impossible to grasp. He felt it in those narrow coffee-coloured bright eagle eyes, slit sideways ; in the alarming curve of the black eyebrows, which sprang upwards from the bridge of the nose ; in the healthy dryness of the skin strained over the huge cheekbones ; and, above all, in the general expression of the face—malicious, sneering, intelligent, perhaps even haughty, but not human, like a wild beast rather, or, more truly, a face belonging to a creature of another planet.

' It 's as if I 'd seen him in a dream ! ' the thought flashed through Schavinsky's brain. While he looked at the face attentively he unconsciously screwed up his eyes, and bent his head sideways.

Ribnikov immediately turned round to him and began to giggle loudly and nervously.

' Why are you admiring me, Mr. Author. Interested ? I ! ' He raised his voice and thumped his chest with a curious pride. ' I am Captain Ribnikov. Rib-ni-kov ! An orthodox Russian warrior who slaughters the enemy, without number. That 's a Russian soldier's song. Eh, what ? '

Kodlubtzov, running his pen over the paper, said carelessly, without looking at Ribnikov, ' and without number, surrenders.'

Ribnikov threw a quick glance at Kodlubtzov, and Schavinsky noticed that strange yellow green fires flashed in his little brown eyes. But this lasted only an instant. The captain giggled, shrugged, and noisily smacked his thighs.

'You can't do anything; it 's the will of the Lord. As the fable says, Set a thief to catch a thief. Eh, what ?'

He suddenly turned to Schavinsky, tapped him lightly on the knee, and with his lips uttered a hopeless sound: 'Phwit! We do everything on the off-chance—higgledy-piggledy—anyhow! We can't adapt ourselves to the terrain; the shells never fit the guns; men in the firing line get nothing to eat for four days. And the Japanese—damn them—work like machines. Yellow monkeys—and civilisation is on their side. Damn them! Eh, what ?'

'So you think they may win ?' Schavinsky asked.

Again Ribnikov's lips twitched. Schavinsky had already managed to notice this habit of his. All through the conversation, especially when the captain asked a question and guardedly waited the answer, or nervously turned to face a fixed glance from some one, his lips would twitch suddenly, first on one side then on the other, and he would make strange grimaces, like convulsive, malignant smiles. At the same time he would hastily lick his dry, cracked lips with the tip of his tongue—thin bluish lips like a monkey's or a goat's.

'Who knows ?' said the captain. 'God only. . . . You can't set foot on your own doorstep without God's help, as the proverb goes. Eh, what ? The campaign isn't over yet. Everything 's still to come. The Russian 's used to victory. Remember Poltava and the unforgettable Suvorov . . . and Sebastopol ! . . . and how we cleared out Napoleon, the greatest captain in the world, in 1812. Great is the God of Russia. What ? '

As he began to talk the corners of his lips twitched into strange smiles, malignant, sneering, inhuman, and an ominous yellow gleam played in his eyes, beneath the black frowning eyebrows.

At that moment they brought Schavinsky coffee.

' Wouldn't you like a glass of cognac ? ' he asked the captain.

Ribnikov again tapped him lightly on the knee. ' No thanks, old man. I 've drunk a frightful lot to-day, damn it. My noddle 's fairly splitting. Damn it all, I 've been pegging since the early morning. " Russia's joy 's in the bottle ! " Eh, what ? ' he cried suddenly, with an air of bravado and an unexpectedly drunken note in his voice.

' He 's shamming,' Schavinsky instantly thought. But for some reason he did not want to leave off, and he went on treating the captain.

' What do you say to beer . . . red wine ? '

' No thanks. I 'm drunk already without that. *Gran' merci*.'

' Have some soda ? '

The captain cheered up.

' Yes, yes, please. Soda, certainly. I could do with a glass.'

They brought a siphon. Ribnikov drank a glass in large greedy gulps. Even his hands began to tremble with eagerness. He poured himself out another immediately. At once it could be seen that he had been suffering a long torment of thirst.

'He 's shamming,' Schavinsky thought again. 'What an amazing man! Excited and tired, but not the least bit drunk.'

'It 's hot—damn it,' Ribnikov said hoarsely. 'But I think, gentlemen, I 'm interfering with your business.'

'No, it 's all right. We 're used to it,' said Riazhkin shortly.

'Haven't you any fresh news of the war?' Ribnikov asked. 'A-ah, gentlemen,' he suddenly cried and banged his sword. 'What a lot of interesting copy I could give you about the war! If you like, I 'll dictate, you need only write. You need only write. Just call it: Reminiscences of Captain Ribnikov, returned from the Front. No, don't imagine—I 'll do it for nothing, free, gratis. What do you say to that, my dear authors?'

'Well, it might be done,' came Matanya's lazy voice from somewhere. 'We 'll manage a little interview for you somehow. Tell me, Vladimir Ivanovich, do you know anything of the Fleet?'

'No, nothing. . . . Is there any news?'

'There 's an incredible story, Kondrashov heard from a friend on the Naval Staff. Hi! Pathological Case! Tell Schavinsky.'

The Pathological Case, a man with a black tragedy beard and a chewed-up face, spoke through his nose:

'I can't guarantee it, Vladimir Ivanovich. But the source seems reliable. There 's a nasty rumour going about the Staff that the great part of our Fleet has surrendered without fighting—that the sailors tied up the officers and ran up the white flag—something like twenty ships.'

'That 's really terrible,' said Schavinsky in a quiet voice. 'Perhaps it 's not true, yet? Still—nowadays, the most impossible things are possible. By the way, do you know what 's happening in the naval ports—in all the ships' crews there 's a terrible underground ferment going on. The naval officers ashore are frightened to meet the men in their command.'

The conversation became general. This inquisitive, ubiquitous, cynical company was a sensitive receiver, unique of its kind, for every conceivable rumour and gossip of the town, which often reached the private saloon of 'The Glory of Petrograd' quicker than the minister's sanctum. Each one had his news. It was so interesting that even the Three Musketeers, who seemed to count nothing in the world sacred or important, began to talk with unusual fervour.

'There 's a rumour going about that the reserves in the rear of the army refuse to obey orders. The soldiers are shooting the officers with their own revolvers.'

'I heard that the general in command hanged

fifty sisters of mercy. Well, of course, they were only dressed as sisters of mercy.'

Schavinsky glanced round at Ribnikov. Now the talkative captain was silent. With his eyes screwed and his chest pressed upon the hilt of his sword, he was intently watching each of the speakers in turn. Under the tight-stretched skin of his cheekbones the sinews strongly played, and his lips moved as if he were repeating every word to himself.

'My God, whom *does* he remind me of?' the journalist thought impatiently for the tenth time. This so tormented him that he tried to make use of an old familiar trick . . . to pretend to himself that he had completely forgotten the captain, and then suddenly to give him a quick glance. Usually that trick soon helped him to recall a name or a meeting-place, but now it was quite ineffective.

Under his stubborn look, Ribnikov turned round again, gave a deep sigh and shook his head sadly.

'Awful news! Do you believe it? What? Even if it is true we need not despair. You know what we Russians say: "Whom God defends the pigs can't eat,"—that's to say, I mean that the pigs are the Japanese, of course.'

He held out stubbornly against Schavinsky's steady look, and in his yellow animal eyes the journalist noticed a flame of implacable, inhuman hatred.

Piestrukhin, the poet asleep on the sofa,

suddenly got up, smacked his lips, and stared at the officer with dazed eyes.

'Ah! . . . you're still here, Jap mug,' he said drunkenly, hardly moving his mouth. 'You just get out of it!'

And he collapsed on the sofa again, turning on to his other side.

'Japanese!' Schavinsky thought with anxious curiosity, '*That's* what he's like,' and drawled meaningly: 'You *are* a jewel, Captain!'

'I?' the latter cried out. His eyes lost their fire, but his lips still twitched nervously. 'I am Captain Ribnikov!' He banged himself on the chest again with curious pride. 'My Russian heart bleeds. Allow me to shake your hand. My head was grazed at Liao-Yang, and I was wounded in the leg at Mukden. You don't believe it? I'll show you now.'

He put his foot on a chair and began to pull up his trousers.

'Don't! . . . stop! we believe you,' Schavinsky said with a frown. Nevertheless, his habitual curiosity enabled him to steal a glance at Ribnikov's leg and to notice that this infantry captain's underclothing was of expensive spun silk.

A messenger came into the saloon with a letter for Matanya.

'That's for you, Vladimir Ivanovich,' said Matanya, when he had torn the envelope. 'The race-card from the stable. Put one on Zenith both ways for me. I'll pay you on Tuesday.'

'Come to the races with me, Captain?' said Schavinsky.

'Where? To the races? With pleasure.' Ribnikov got up noisily, upsetting his chair. 'Where the horses jump? Captain Ribnikov at your service. Into battle, on the march, to the devil's dam! Ha, ha, ha! That's me! Eh, what?'

When they were sitting in the cab, driving through Cabinetsky Street, Schavinsky slipped his arm through the officer's, bent right down to his ear, and said, in a voice hardly audible:

'Don't be afraid. I shan't betray you. You're as much Ribnikov as I am Vanderbilt. You're an officer on the Japanese Staff. I think you're a colonel at least, and now you're a military agent in Russia. . . .'

Either Ribnikov did not hear the words for the noise of the wheels or he did not understand. Swaying gently from side to side, he spoke hoarsely with a fresh drunken enthusiasm:

'We're fairly on the spree now! Damn it all, I adore it. I'm not Captain Ribnikov, a Russian soldier, if I don't love Russian writers! A magnificent lot of fellows! They drink like fishes, and know all about life. "Russia's joy is in the bottle." And I've been at it from the morning, old man!'

III

By business and disposition Schavinsky was a collector of human documents, of rare and strange manifestations of the human spirit. Often for weeks, sometimes for months together, he watched an interesting type, tracking him down with the persistence of a passionate sportsman or an eager detective. It would happen that the prize was found to be, as he called it, 'a knight of the black star'—a sharper, a notorious plagiarist, a pimp, a souteneur, a literary maniac, the terror of every editor, a plunging cashier or bank messenger, who spends public money in restaurants and gambling hells with the madness of a man rushing down the steep; but no less the objects of his sporting passion were the lions of the season—pianists, singers, littérateurs, gamblers with amazing luck, jockeys, athletes, and cocottes coming into vogue. By hook or crook Schavinsky made their acquaintance and then, enveloping them in his spider's toils, tenderly and gently secured his victim's attention. Then he was ready for anything. He would sit for whole sleepless nights with vulgar, stupid people, whose mental equipment, like the Hottentots', consisted of a dozen or two animal conceptions and clichés; he stood drinks and dinners to damnable fools and scoundrels, waiting patiently for the moment when in their drunkenness they would reveal the full flower of their villainy. He flattered them to the top of their bent, with his eyes open; gave them monstrous doses of flattery, firmly convinced that flattery is the key to open every lock; he lent them money generously, knowing well that he would never receive it back again. In justification of this precarious sport he could say that the inner psychological interest for him considerably surpassed the benefits he subsequently acquired as a realistic writer. It gave him a subtle and obscure delight to penetrate into the mysterious inaccessible chambers of the human soul, to observe the hidden springs of external acts, springs sometimes petty, sometimes shameful, more often ridiculous than affecting—as it were, to hold in his hand for a while, a live, warm human heart and touch its very pulse. Often in this inquisitive pursuit it seemed to him that he was completely losing his own 'ego,' so much did he begin to think and feel with another's soul, even speaking in his language with his peculiar words until at last he even caught himself using another's gesture and tone. But when he had saturated himself in a man he threw him aside. It is true that sometimes he had to pay long and heavily for a moment's infatuation.

But no one for a long time had so deeply interested him, even to agitation, as this hoarse, tippling infantry captain. For a whole day Schavinsky did not let him go. As he sat by his side in the cab and watched him surreptitiously, Schavinsky resolved:

'No, I can't be mistaken;—this yellow, squinting face with the cheekbones, these eternal bobs and bows, and the incessant hand washing; above all this strained, nervous, uneasy familiarity. . . . But if it 's all true, and Captain Ribnikov is really a Japanese spy, then what extraordinary presence of mind the man must have to play with this magnificent audacity, this diabolically true caricature of a broken-down officer in broad daylight in a hostile capital. What awful sensations he must have, balanced every second of the day on the very edge of certain death!'

Here was something completely inexplicable to Schavinsky—a fascinating, mad, cool audacity—perhaps the very noblest kind of patriotic devotion. An acute curiosity, together with a reverent fear, drew the journalist's mind more and more strongly towards the soul of this amazing captain.

But sometimes he pulled himself up mentally: 'Suppose I 've forced myself to believe in a ridiculous preconceived idea? Suppose I 've just let myself be fooled by a disreputable captain in my inquisitive eagerness to read men's souls? Surely there are any number of yellow Mongol faces in the Ural or among the Oremburg Cossacks.' Still more intently he looked into every motion and expression of the captain's face, listened intently to every sound of his voice.

Ribnikov did not miss a single soldier who

gave him a salute as he passed. He put his hand to the peak of his cap with a peculiarly prolonged and exaggerated care. Whenever they drove past a church he invariably raised his hat and crossed himself punctiliously with a broad sweep of his arm, and as he did it he gave an almost imperceptible side-glance to his companion—is he noticing or not ?

Once Schavinsky could hold out no longer, and said: 'But you 're pious, though, Captain.'

Ribnikov threw out his hands, hunched his shoulders up funnily, and said in his hoarse voice: 'Can't be helped, old man. I 've got the habit of it at the Front. The man who fights learns to pray, you know. It 's a splendid Russian proverb. You learn to say your prayers out there, whether you like it or not. You go into the firing line. The bullets are whirring, terribly—shrapnel, bombs . . . those cursed Japanese shells. . . . But it can't be helped—duty, your oath, and off you go! And you say to yourself: "Our Father, which art in heaven, hallowed be Thy name. Thy kingdom come. Thy Will be done in earth, as it is in heaven . . ."'

And he said the whole prayer to the end, carefully shaping out each sound.

'Spy!' Schavinsky decided.

But he would not leave his suspicion halfway. For hours on end he went on watching and goading the captain. In a private room of a restaurant at dinner he bent right over the table and looked into Ribnikov's very pupils.

'Listen, Captain. No one can hear us now. . . . What 's the strongest oath I can give you that no one will ever hear of our conversation? . . . I 'm convinced, absolutely and beyond all doubt, that you 're a Japanese.'

Ribnikov banged himself on the chest again.

'I am Capt——'

'No, no. Let 's have done with these tricks. You can't hide your face, however clever you are. The line of your cheekbones, the cut of your eyes, your peculiar head, the colour of your skin, the stiff, straggling growth on your face—everything points beyond all shadow of doubt to you belonging to the yellow race. But you 're safe. I shan't tell on you, whatever offers they make me, however they threaten me for silence. I shan't do you any harm, if it 's only because I 'm full of admiration for your amazing courage. I say more—I 'm full of reverence, terror if you like. I 'm a writer—that 's a man of fancy and imagination. I can't even imagine how it 's possible for a man to make up his mind to it: to come thousands of miles from your country to a city full of enemies that hate you, risking your life every second—you 'll be hanged without a trial if you 're caught, I suppose you know? And then to go walking about in an officer's uniform, to enter every possible kind of company, and hold the most dangerous conversations. The least mistake, one slip will ruin you in a second. Half an hour ago you used the word " holograph " instead of " manuscript." A trifle, but very characteristic. An army captain would never use this word of a modern manuscript, but only of an archive or a very solemn document. He wouldn't even say " manuscript," but just a " book "—but these are trifles. But the one thing I don't understand is the incessant strain of the mind and will, the diabolical waste of spiritual strength. To forget to think in Japanese, to forget your name utterly, to identify yourself completely with another's personality—no, this is surely greater than any heroism they told us of in school. My dear man, don't try to play with me. I swear I 'm not your enemy.'

He said all this quite sincerely, for his whole being was stirred to flame by the heroic picture of his imagination. But the captain would not let himself be flattered. He listened to him, and stared with eyes slightly closed at his glass, which he quietly moved over the tablecloth, and the corners of his blue lips twisted nervously. And in his face Schavinsky recognised the same hidden mockery, the same deep, stubborn, implacable hatred, the peculiar hatred that a European can perhaps never understand, felt by a wise, cultured, civilised beast, made man, for a being of another species.

'Keep your kindness in your pocket,' replied Ribnikov carelessly. 'Let it go to hell. They teased me in the regiment too with being a Jap. Chuck it! I 'm Captain Ribnikov. You know there 's a Russian proverb, " The face of a beast with the soul of a man." I 'll just tell you there was once a case in our regiment——'

'What was your regiment ?' Schavinsky asked suddenly.

But the captain seemed not to have heard. He began to tell the old, threadbare dirty stories that are told in camp, on manœuvres, and in barracks, and in spite of himself Schavinsky began to feel insulted. Once during the evening as they sat in the cab Schavinsky put his arm round his waist, and drew him close and said in a low voice :

'Captain . . . no, Colonel, at least, or you would never have been given such a serious mission. Let 's say Colonel, then. I do homage to your daring, that is to the boundless courage of the Japanese nation. Sometimes when I read or think of individual cases of your diabolical bravery and contempt of death, I tremble with ecstasy. What immortal beauty, what divine courage there is, for instance, in the action of the captain of the shattered warship who answered the call to surrender by quietly lighting a cigarette, and went to the bottom with a cigarette in his lips ! What titanic strength, what thrilling contempt for the enemy ! And the naval cadets on the fireships who went to certain death, delighted as though they were going to a ball ! And do you remember how a lieutenant, all by himself, towed a torpedo in a boat at night to make an end of the mole at Port Arthur ? The searchlights were turned on and all there remained of the lieutenant and his boat was a bloody stain on the concrete wall. But the next day all the midshipmen and lieutenants of the Japanese Fleet overwhelmed Admiral Togo with applications, offering to repeat the exploit. What amazing heroes! But still more magnificent is Togo's order that the officers under him should not so madly risk their lives, which belong to their country and not to them. It's damnably beautiful, though!'

'What's this street we're in?' interrupted Ribnikov, yawning. 'After the dug-outs in Manchuria I've completely lost my sense of direction in the street. When we were in Kharbin. . . .'

But the ecstatic Schavinsky went on, without listening to him.

'Do you remember the case of an officer who was taken prisoner and battered his head to pieces on a stone? But the most wonderful thing is the signatures of the Samurai. Of course, you've never heard of it, Captain Ribnikov?' Schavinsky asked with sarcastic emphasis. 'It's understood, you haven't heard of it. . . . You see General Nogi asked for volunteers to march in the leading column in a night attack on the Port Arthur forts. Nearly the whole brigade offered themselves for this honourable death. Since there were too many and they pressed in front of each other for the opportunity of death, they had to make application in writing, and some of them, according to an old custom, cut off the first finger of their left hand and fixed it to their signature for a seal of blood. That 's what the Samurai did ! '

' Samurai,' Ribnikov dully repeated. There was a noise in his throat as if something had snapped and spread. Schavinsky gave a quick glance to his profile. An expression such as he had never seen in the captain's face before suddenly played about his mouth and on his chin, which trembled once ; and his eyes began to shine with the warm, tremulous light which gleams through sudden, brimming tears. But he pulled himself together instantly, shut his eyes for a second, and turned a naïve and stupid face to Schavinsky, and suddenly uttered a long, filthy, Russian oath.

' Captain, Captain, what 's the matter with you ? ' Schavinsky cried, almost in fright.

' That 's all newspaper lies,' Ribnikov said unconcernedly. ' Our Russian Tommy is not a bit behind. There 's a difference, of course. They fight for their life, however, independence —and what have we mixed ourselves up in it for ? Nobody knows ! The devil alone knows why. "There was no sorrow till the devil pumped it up," as we say in Russian. What ! Ha, ha, ha ! '

On the race-course the sport distracted Schavinsky's attention a little, and he could not observe the captain all the while. But in the intervals between the events, he saw him every now and then in one or another of the stands, upstairs or downstairs, in the buffet or by the *pari-mutuel.* That day the word Tsushima was on everybody's lips—backers, jockeys, bookmakers, even the mysterious, ragged beings that are inevitable on every race-course. The word was used to jeer at a beaten horse, by men who were annoyed at losing, with indifferent laughter and with bitterness. Here and there it was uttered with passion. Schavinsky saw from a distance how the captain in his easy, confident way picked a quarrel with one man, shook hands with others, and tapped others on the shoulder. His small, limping figure appeared and disappeared everywhere.

From the races they drove to a restaurant, and from there to Schavinsky's house. The journalist was rather ashamed of his rôle of voluntary detective; but he felt it was out of his power to throw it up, though he had already begun to feel tired, and his head ached with the strain of this stealthy struggle with another man's soul. Convinced that flattery had been of no avail, he now tried to draw the captain to frankness, by teasing and rousing his feelings of patriotism.

'Still, I'm sorry for these poor Japs,' he said with ironical pity. 'When all is said, Japan has exhausted all her national genius in this war. In my opinion she's like a feeble little man who lifts a half dozen hundredweight on his shoulders, either in ecstasy or intoxication, or out of mere bravado, and strains his insides, and is already beginning to die a lingering death. You see Russia's an entirely different country.

She's a Colossus. To her the Manchurian defeats are just the same as cupping a full-blooded man. You'll see how she will recover and begin to blossom when the war is over. But Japan will wither and die. She's strained herself. Don't tell me they have civilisation, universal education, European technique: at the end of it all, a Japanese is an Asiatic, half-man, half-monkey. Even in type he approaches a Bushman, a Touareg, or a Blackfellow. You have only to look at his facial angle. It all comes to this, they're just Japs! It wasn't your civilisation or your political youth that conquered us at all, but simply a fit of madness. Do you know what a seizure is, a fit of frenzy? A feeble woman tears chains to pieces and tosses strong men about like straws. The next day she hasn't even the power to lift her hand. It's the same with Japan. Believe me, after the heroic fit will follow impotence and decay; but certainly before that she will pass through a stage of national swagger, outrageous militarism and insane Chauvinism.'

'Really?' cried Ribnikov in stupid rapture. 'You can't get away from the truth. Shake hands, Mr. Author. You can always tell a clever man at once.'

He laughed hoarsely, spat about, tapped Schavinsky's knee, and shook his hand, and Schavinsky suddenly felt ashamed of himself and the tricks of his stealthy searching into human souls.

'What if I'm mistaken and this Ribnikov is

only the truest type of the drunken infantry-man. No, it 's impossible. But if it is possible, then what a fool I 'm making of myself, my God ! '

At his house he showed the captain his library, his rare engravings, a collection of old china, and a couple of small Siberian dogs. His wife, who played small parts in musical comedy, was out of town. Ribnikov examined everything with a polite, uninterested curiosity, in which his host caught something like boredom, and even cold contempt. Ribnikov casually opened a magazine and read some lines aloud.

' He 's made a blunder now,' Schavinsky thought, when he heard his extraordinary correct and wooden reading, each separate letter pronounced with exaggerated precision like the head boy in a French class showing off. Evidently Ribnikov noticed it himself, for he soon shut the book and asked :

' But you 're a writer yourself ? '

' Yes. . . . I do a bit.'

' What newspapers do you write for ? '

Schavinsky named them. It was the sixth time he had been asked the question that day.

' Oh, yes, yes, yes. I forgot, I 've asked you before. D' you know what, Mr. Author ? '

' What is it ? '

' Let us do this. You write and I 'll dictate. That is, I won't dictate . . . oh, no, I shall never dare.' Ribnikov rubbed his hands and bowed hurriedly. ' You 'll compose it yourself, of course. I 'll only give you some thoughts and—what shall I call them—reminiscences of the war? Oh, what a lot of interesting copy I have! . . .'

Schavinsky sat sideways on the table and glanced at the captain, cunningly screwing up one eye.

'Of course, I shall give your name?'

'Why, you may. I 've no objection. Put it like this: "This information was supplied to me by Captain Ribnikov who has just returned from the Front."'

'Very well. Why do you want this?'

'What?'

'Having your name in it. Do you want it for future evidence that you inspired the Russian newspapers? What a clever fellow, I am, eh?'

But the captain avoided a direct answer, as usual.

'But perhaps you haven't time? You are engaged in other work. Well, let the reminiscences go to hell! You won't be able to tell the whole story. As they say: "There 's a difference between living a life and crossing a field." Eh, what? Ha, ha, ha!'

An interesting fancy came into Schavinsky's head. In his study stood a big, white table of unpainted ash. On the clean virgin surface of this table all Schavinsky's friends used to leave their autographs in the shape of aphorisms, verses, drawings, and even notes of music. He said to Ribnikov: 'See, here is my autograph-book, Captain. Won't you write me something in memory of our pleasant meeting, and our acquaintance which'—Schavinsky bowed politely—'I venture to hope will not be short-lived?'

'With pleasure,' Ribnikov readily agreed. 'Something from Pushkin or Gogol?'

'No . . . far better something of your own.'

'Of my own? Splendid.'

He took the pen and dipped it, thought and prepared to write, but Schavinsky suddenly stopped him.

'We'd better do this. Here's a piece of a paper. There are drawing-pins in the box at the corner. Please write something particularly interesting and then cover it with the paper and fasten the corners with the drawing-pins. I give you my word of honour as an author, that for two months I won't put a finger on the paper and won't look at what you've written. Is that all right? Well, write then. I'll go out of the room so as not to hinder you.'

After five minutes Ribnikov shouted to him: 'Please come in.'

'Ready?' Schavinsky asked, entering.

Ribnikov drew himself up, put his hand to his forehead in salute and shouted like a soldier: 'Very good, sir.'

'Thanks. Now we'll go to the "Buff," or somewhere else,' Schavinsky said. 'There we'll think what we'll do next. I shan't let you out of my sight to-day, Captain.'

'With the greatest pleasure,' Ribnikov said in a hoarse bass, clicking his heels. He lifted up his shoulders and gave a military twist to his moustaches on either side.

But Schavinsky, against his own will, did not keep his word. At the last moment before leaving his house the journalist remembered that he had left his cigarette-case in the study and went back for it, leaving Ribnikov in the hall. The piece of white paper, carefully fastened with drawing-pins, aroused his curiosity. He could not resist the temptation ; he turned back stealthily and after lifting a corner of the paper quickly read the words written in a thin, distinct and extraordinary elegant hand :

'Though you are Ivanov the seventh, you 're a fool all the same.'

IV

LONG after midnight they were coming out of a suburban café chantant accompanied by the well-known musical comedy actor Zhenin-Lirsky, the young assistant Crown-Prosecutor Sashka Strahlmann, who was famous all over Petersburg for his incomparable skill in telling amusing stories about the topic of the day, and Karyukov, the merchant's son, a patron of the arts.

It was neither bright nor dark. It was a warm, white, transparent night, with soft *chatoyant* colours and water like mother-of-pearl in the calm canals, which plainly reflected the grey stone of the quay and the motionless foliage of the trees. The sky was pale as though tired and sleepless, and there were sleepy clouds in the sky, long, thin and woolly like clews of ravelled cotton-wool.

'Where shall we go, now?' said Schavinsky, stopping at the gate of the gardens. 'Field-Marshal Oyama! Give us your enlightened opinion.'

All five lingered on the pavement for a while, caught by a moment of the usual early morning indecision, when the physical fatigue of the reveller struggles with the irresistible and irritating yearning after new and piquant sensations. From the garden continually came patrons, laughing, whistling, noisily shuffling their feet over the dry, white cobble-stones. Walking hurriedly, boldly rustling the silk of their petticoats emerged the *artistes* wearing huge hats, with diamonds trembling in their ears, escorted by dashing gentlemen, smartly dressed, with flowers in their buttonholes. With the porters' respectful assistance these ladies fluttered into carriages and panting automobiles, freely arranging their dresses round their legs, and flew away holding the brims of their hats in their hands. The chorus-girls and the *filles du jardin* of the higher class drove off alone or two together in ordinary cabs with a man beside them. The ordinary women of the street appeared everywhere at once, going round the wooden fence, following close on the men who left on foot, giving special attention to the drunken. They ran beside the men for a long while, offering themselves in a whisper with impudent submissiveness, naming that which was their profession with blunt, coarse, terrible words. In the bright, white twilight of May, their faces seemed like coarse masks, blue from the white of their complexions, red with crimson colour, and one's eyes were struck with the blackness, the thickness and the extraordinary curve of their eyebrows. These naïvely bright colours made the yellow of their wrinkled temples appear all the more pitiable, their thin, scraggy necks, and flabby, feeble chins. A couple of mounted policemen, obscenely swearing, rode them down now and then with their horses' mouths afoam. The girls screamed, ran away, and clutched at the sleeves of the passers-by. Near the railing of the canal was gathered a group of about twenty men—it was the usual early morning scandal. A short, beardless boy of an officer was dead-drunk and making a fuss, looking as though he wanted to draw his sword; a policeman was assuring him of something in a convincing falsetto with his hand on his heart.

A sharp, suspicious-looking type, drunk, in a cap with a ragged peak, spoke in a sugary, obsequious voice: 'Spit on 'em, yer honour. They ain't worth looking at. Give me one in the jaw, if you like. Allow me to kiss yer 'and.'

A thin, stern gentleman at the back, whose thick, black whiskers could alone be seen, because his bowler was tilted over his face, drawled in a low, indistinct voice: 'What do you stand about talking for? Pitch him into the water and have done with it!'

'But really, Major Fukushima,' said the actor, 'we must put a decent finish to the day of our pleasant acquaintance. Let 's go off with the little ladies. Where shall it be, Sashka?'

'Bertha?' Strahlmann asked in reply.

Ribnikov giggled and rubbed his hands in joyful agitation.

'Women? "Even a Jew hanged himself for company's sake," as the Russian proverb says. Where the world goes there go we. Eh, what? "If we 're going, let 's go," as the parrot said. What? Ha, ha, ha!'

Schavinsky had introduced him to the young men, and they had all had supper in the café chantant, listened to the Roumanian singers, drinking champagne and liqueurs. At one time they found it amusing to call Ribnikov by the names of different Japanese generals, particularly because the captain's good nature was evidently unlimited. Schavinsky it was who began this rude, familiar game. True he felt at times that he was behaving in an ugly, perhaps even treacherous, way to Ribnikov, but he calmed his conscience by the fact that he had not breathed a word of his suspicions, which never entered his friends' heads at all.

At the beginning of the evening he was watching Ribnikov. The captain was noisier and more talkative than anybody: he was incessantly drinking healths, jumping up, sitting down, pouring the wine over the tablecloth, lighting his cigarette the wrong end. Nevertheless, Schavinsky noticed that he was drinking very little.

Ribnikov had to sit next the journalist again in the cab. Schavinsky was almost sober. He was generally distinguished for a hard head in a spree, but it was light and noisy now, as though the foam of the champagne was bubbling in it. He gave the captain a side-glance. In the uncertain, drowsy light of the white night Ribnikov's face wore a dark, earthy complexion. All the hollows were sharp and black, the little wrinkles on his forehead and the lines round his nose and mouth were deepened. The captain himself sat with a weary stoop, his hands tucked into the sleeves of his uniform, breathing heavily through his open mouth. Altogether it gave him a worn, suffering look. Schavinsky could even smell his breath, and thought that gamblers after several nights at cards have just the same stale, sour breath as men tired out with insomnia or the strain of long brain work. A wave of kindly emotion and pity welled up in Schavinsky's heart. The captain suddenly appeared to him very small, utterly worn out, affecting and pitiable. He embraced Ribnikov, drew him close, and said affably: 'Very well, Captain, I surrender. I can't do anything with you, and I apologise if I've given you some uncomfortable minutes. Give me your hand.'

He unfastened the rose he wore in his coat which a girl in the garden had made him buy, and fixed it in the buttonhole of the captain's great-coat.

'This is my peace-offering, Captain. We won't tease each other any more.'

The cab drew up at a two-storied stone house standing apart in a pleasant approach. All the windows were shuttered. The others had gone in advance and were waiting for them. A square grille, a handsbreadth wide, set in the heavy door, was opened from inside, and a pair of cold, searching grey eyes appeared in it for a few seconds. Then the door was opened.

This establishment was something between an expensive brothel and a luxurious club.

There was an elegant entrance, a stuffed bear in the hall, carpets, silk curtains and lustre-chandeliers, and lackeys in evening dress and white gloves. Men came here to finish the night after the restaurants were shut. Cards were played, expensive wines kept, and there was always a generous supply of fresh, pretty women who were often changed.

They had to go up to the first floor, where was a wide landing adorned by palms in tubs and separated from the stairs by a balustrade. Schavinsky went upstairs arm-in-arm with Ribnikov. Though he had promised himself that he would not tease him any more, he could not restrain himself: 'Let 's mount the scaffold, Captain!'

'I 'm not afraid,' said he lazily. 'I walk up to death every day of my life.'

Ribnikov waved his hand feebly and smiled with constraint. The smile made his face suddenly weary, grey and old.

Schavinsky gave him a look of silent surprise. He was ashamed of his importunity. But Ribnikov passed it off immediately.

'Yes, to death . . . A soldier 's always ready for it. There 's nothing to be done. Death is the trifling inconvenience attached to our profession.'

Schavinsky and Karyukov the art-patron were assiduous guests and honoured *habitués* of the house. They were greeted with pleasant smiles and low bows.

A big, warm *cabinet* was given them, in red

and gold with a thick, bright green carpet on the floor, with sconces in the corners and on the table. They were brought champagne, fruit and bonbons. Women came—three at first, then two more—then they were passing in and out continually. Without exception they were pretty, well provided with bare, white arms, neck, bosom, in bright, expensive, glittering dresses. Some wore ballet skirts ; one was in a schoolgirl's brown uniform, another in tight riding-breeches and a jockey's cap. A stout elderly lady in black also came, rather like a landlady or a housekeeper. Her appearance was decent ; her face flabby and yellow. She laughed continually the pleasant laugh of an elderly woman, coughed continually and smoked incessantly. She behaved to Schavinsky, the actor, and the art-patron with the unconstrained *coquetterie* of a lady old enough to be their mother, flicking their hands with her handkerchief, and she called Strahlmann, who was evidently her favourite, Sashka.

'General Kuroki, let 's drink to the success of the grand Manchurian army. You 'll be getting mildewy, sitting in your corner,' said Karyukov.

Schavinsky interrupted him with a yawn: 'Steady, gentlemen. I think you ought to be bored with it by now. You 're just abusing the captain's good nature.'

'I 'm not offended,' replied Ribnikov. 'Gentlemen ! Let us drink the health of our charming ladies.'

'Sing us something, Lirsky!' Schavinsky asked.

The actor cheerfully sat down to the piano and began a gipsy song. It was more recitation than singing. He never moved the cigar from his lips, stared at the ceiling, with a parade of swinging to and fro on his chair. The women joined in, loud and out of tune. Each one tried to race the others with the words. Then Sashka Strahlmann gave an admirable imitation of a gramophone, impersonated an Italian opera, and mimicked animals. Karyukov danced a fandango and called for bottle after bottle.

He was the first to disappear from the room, with a red-haired Polish girl. After him followed Strahlmann and the actor. Only Schavinsky remained, with a swarthy, white-toothed Hungarian girl on his knees, and Ribnikov, by the side of a tall blonde in a blue satin blouse, cut square and open half-way down her breast.

'Well, Captain, let's say good-bye for a little while,' said Schavinsky, getting up and stretching himself. 'It's late—we'd better say early. Come and have breakfast with me at one o'clock, Captain. Put the wine down to Karyukov, Madame. If he loves sacred art, then he can pay for the honour of having supper with its priests. *Mes compliments!*'

The blonde put her bare arm round the captain's neck and kissed him, and said simply: 'Let us go too, darling. It really is late.'

V

SHE had a little gay room with a bright blue paper, a pale blue hanging lamp. On the toilet-table stood a round mirror in a frame of light blue satin. There were two oleographs on one wall, 'Girls Bathing' and 'The Royal Bridegroom,' on the other a hanging, with a wide brass bed alongside.

The woman undressed, and with a sense of pleasant relief passed her hands over her body, where her chemise had been folded under her corset. Then she turned the lamp down and sat on the bed, and began calmly to unlace her boots.

Ribnikov sat by the table with his elbows apart and his head resting in his hands. He could not tear his eyes from her big, handsome legs and plump calves, which her black, transparent stockings so closely fitted.

'Why don't you undress, officer?' the woman asked. 'Tell me, darling, why do they call you Japanese General?'

Ribnikov gave a laugh, with his eyes still fixed upon her legs.

'Oh, it's just nonsense. Only a joke. Do you know the verses:

"It hardly can be called a sin,
If something's funny and you grin! . . ."'

'Will you stand me some champagne, darling. . . . Since you 're so stingy, oranges will do. Are you going soon or staying the night ?'

'Staying the night. Come to me.'

She lay down with him, hastily threw her cigarette over on to the floor and wriggled beneath the blanket.

'Do you like to be next to the wall ?' she asked. 'Do if you want to. O-oh, how cold your legs are ! You know I love army men. What 's your name ?'

'Mine ?' He coughed and answered in an uncertain tone: 'I am Captain Ribnikov. Vassily Alexandrovich Ribnikov !'

'Ah, Vasya ! I have a friend called Vasya, a little chap from the Lycée. Oh, what a darling he is !'

She began to sing, pretending to shiver under the bedclothes, laughing and half-closing her eyes:

'"Vasya, Vasya, Vasinke,
It 's a tale you 're telling me."

'You *are* like a Japanese, you know, by Jove. Do you know who ? The Mikado. We take in the *Niva* and there 's a picture of him there. It 's late now—else I 'd get it to show you. You 're as like as two peas.'

'I 'm very glad,' said Ribnikov, quietly kissing her smooth, round shoulder.

'Perhaps you 're really a Japanese ? They say you 've been at the war. Is it true ? O-oh, darling, I 'm afraid of being tickled— Is it dreadful at the war ?'

'Dreadful . . . no, not particularly. . . . Don't let 's talk about it,' he said wearily. 'What 's your name ?'

'Clotilde. . . . No, I 'll tell you a secret. My name 's Nastya. They only called me Clotilde here because my name 's so ugly. Nastya, Nastasya—sounds like a cook.'

'Nastya,' he repeated musingly, and cautiously kissed her breast. 'No, it 's a nice name. Na—stya,' he repeated slowly.

'What is there nice about it ? Malvina, Wanda, Zhenia, they 're nice names—especially Irma. . . . Oh, darling,' and she pressed close to him. 'You are a dear . . . so dark. I love dark men. You 're married, surely ?'

'No, I 'm not.'

'Oh, tell us another. Every one here says he's a bachelor. You 've got six children for sure!'

It was dark in the room, for the windows were shuttered and the lamp hardly burned. Her face was quite close to his head, and showed fantastic and changing on the dim whiteness of the pillow. Already it was different from the simple, handsome, round grey-eyed, Russian face of before. It seemed to have grown thinner, and, strangely changing its expression every minute, seemed now tender, kind, mysterious. It reminded Ribnikov of some one infinitely familiar, long beloved, beautiful and fascinating.

'How beautiful you are !' he murmured. 'I love you. . . . I love you. . . .'

He suddenly uttered an unintelligible word, completely foreign to the woman's ear.

'What did you say?' she asked in surprise.

'Nothing. . . . Nothing. . . . Nothing at all. . . . My dear! Dear woman . . . you are a woman . . . I love you. . . .'

He kissed her arms, her neck, trembling with impatience, which it gave him wonderful delight to suppress. He was possessed by a tender and tempestuous passion for the well-fed, childless woman, for her big young body, so cared for and beautiful. His longing for woman had been till now suppressed by his austere, ascetic life, his constant weariness, by the intense exertion of his mind and will: now it devoured him suddenly with an intolerable, intoxicating flame.

'Your hands are cold,' she said, awkward and shy. In this man was something strange and alarming which she could in no way understand. 'Cold hands and a warm heart.'

'Yes, yes, yes. . . . My heart,' he repeated it like a madman, 'My heart is warm, my heart . . .'

Long ago she had grown used to the outward rites and the shameful details of love; she performed them several times every day—mechanically, indifferently, and often with silent disgust. Hundreds of men, from the aged and old, who put their teeth in a glass of water for the night, to youngsters whose voice was only beginning to break and was bass and soprano at once, civilians, army men, priests in mufti, baldheads and men overgrown with hair from head to foot like monkeys, excited and impotent, morphomaniacs who did not conceal their vice from her, beaux, cripples, rakes, who sometimes nauseated her, boys who cried for the bitterness of their first fall—they all embraced her with shameful words, with long kisses, breathed into her face, moaned in the paroxysm of animal passion, which, she knew beforehand, would then and there be changed to unconcealed and insuperable disgust. Long ago all men's faces had in her eyes lost every individual trait—as though they had united into one lascivious, inevitable face, eternally bent over her, the face of a he-goat with stubbly, slobbering lips, clouded eyes, dimmed like frosted glass, distorted and disfigured by a voluptuous grimace, which sickened her because she never shared it.

Besides, they were all rude, exacting and devoid of the elements of shame. They were ludicrously ugly, as only the modern man can be in his underclothes. But this elderly little officer made a new, peculiar, attractive impression on her. His every movement was distinguished by a gentle, insinuating discretion. His kiss, his caress, and his touch were strangely gentle. At the same time he surrounded her imperceptibly with the nervous atmosphere of real and intense passion which even from a distance and against her will arouses a woman's sensuality, makes her docile, and subject to the male's desire. But her poor little mind had never passed beyond the round of everyday life in the house, and could not perceive this strange and agitating spell. She could only whisper shyly, happy and surprised, the usual trivial words:

'What a nice man you are! You're my sweet, aren't you?'

She got up, put the lamp out, and lay beside him again. Through the chinks between the shutters and the wall showed thin threads of the whitening dawn, which filled the room with a misty blue half-light. Behind the partition, somewhere an alarm-clock hurriedly rang. Far away some one was singing sadly in the distance.

'When will you come again?' the woman asked.

'What?' Ribnikov asked sleepily, opening his eyes. 'When am I coming? Soon—to-morrow. . . .'

'I know all about that. Tell me the truth. When are you coming? I'll be lonely without you.'

'M'm. . . . We will come and be alone. . . . We will write to them. They will stay in the mountains . . .' he murmured incoherently.

A heavy slumber enlocked his body; but, as always with men who have long deprived themselves of sleep, he could not sleep at once. No sooner was his consciousness overcast with the soft, dark, delightful cloud of oblivion than his body was shaken by a terrible inward shock. He moaned and shuddered, opened his eyes wide in wild terror, and straightway plunged into an irritating, transitory state between sleep and wakefulness, like a delirium crowded with threatening and confused visions.

The woman had no desire to sleep. She sat up in bed in her chemise, clasping her bended knees with her bare arms, and looked at Ribnikov with timid curiosity. In the bluish half-light his face grew sharper still and yellower, like the face of a dead man. His mouth stood open, but she could not hear his breathing. All over his face, especially about the eyes and mouth, was an expression of such utter weariness and profound human suffering as she had never seen in her life before. She gently passed her hand back over his stiff hair and forehead. The skin was cold and covered all over with clammy sweat. Ribnikov trembled at the touch, cried out in terror, and with a quick movement raised himself from the pillow.

'Ah! Who 's that, who ?' he cried abruptly, wiping his face with his shirt-sleeve.

'What 's the matter, darling ?' the woman asked with sympathy. 'You 're not well ? Shall I get you some water ?'

But Ribnikov had mastered himself, and lay down once more.

'Thanks. It 's all right now. I was dreaming. . . . Go to sleep, dear, do.'

'When do you want me to wake you, darling ?' she asked.

'Wake. . . . In the morning. . . . The sun will rise early. . . . And the horsemen will come. . . . We will go in a boat. . . . And sail over the river. . . .' He was silent and lay quiet for some minutes. Suddenly his still, dead face was distorted with terrible pain. He turned on his back with a moan, and there came in a stream from his lips mysterious, wild-sounding words of a strange language.

The woman held her breath and listened, possessed by the superstitious terror which always comes from a sleeper's delirium. His face was only a couple of inches from hers, and she could not tear her eyes away. He was silent for a while and then began to speak again, many words and unintelligible. Then he was silent again, as though listening attentively to some one's speech. Suddenly the woman heard the only Japanese word she knew, from the newspapers, pronounced aloud with a firm, clear voice :

'Banzai !'

Her heart beat so violently that the velvet coverlet lifted again and again with the throbbing. She remembered how they had called Ribnikov by the names of Japanese generals in the red *cabinet* that day, and a far faint suspicion began to stir in the obscurity of her mind.

Some one lightly tapped on the door. She got up and opened.

'Clotilde dear, is that you ?' a woman's gentle whisper was heard. 'Aren't you asleep ? Come in to me for a moment. Leonka 's with me, and he 's standing some apricot wine. Come on, dear !'

It was Sonya, the Karaim,[1] Clotilde's neigh-

[1] The Karaim are Jews of the pure original stock who entered Russia long before the main immigration and settled in the Crimea. They are free from the ordinary Jewish restrictions.

bour, bound to her by the cloying, hysterical affection which always pairs off the women in these establishments.

'All right. I 'll come now. Oh, I 've something very interesting to tell you. Wait a second. I 'll dress.'

'Nonsense. Don't. Who are you nervous about ? Leonka ? Come, just as you are ! '

She began to put on her petticoat.

Ribnikov roused out of sleep.

'Where are you going to ? ' he asked drowsily.

'Only a minute . . . Back immediately . . . I must . . .' she answered, hurriedly tying the tape round her waist. 'You go to sleep. I 'll be back in a second.'

He had not heard her last words. A dark heavy sleep had instantly engulfed him.

VI

LEONKA was the idol of the whole establishment, beginning with Madame, and descending to the tiniest servant. In these places where boredom, indolence, and cheap literature produce feverishly romantic tastes, the extreme of adoration is lavished on thieves and detectives, because of their heroic lives, which are full of fascinating risks, dangers and adventures. Leonka used to appear in the most varied costumes, at times almost made up. Sometimes he kept a meaning and mysterious silence. Above all every one remembered very well that he often proclaimed that the local police had an unbounded respect for him and fulfilled his orders blindly. In one case he had said three or four words in a mysterious jargon, and that was enough to send a few thieves who were behaving rowdily in the house crawling into the street. Besides there were times when he had a great deal of money. It is easy to understand that Henrietta, whom he called Genka and with whom he had an assiduous affair, was treated with a jealous respect.

He was a young man with a swarthy, freckled face, with black moustaches that pointed up to his very eyes. His chin was short, firm and broad; his eyes were dark, handsome and impudent. He was sitting on the sofa in his shirt-sleeves, his waistcoat unbuttoned and his necktie loose. He was small but well proportioned. His broad chest and his muscles, so big that his shirt seemed ready to tear at the shoulder, were eloquent of his strength. Genka sat close to him with her feet on the sofa; Clotilde was opposite. Sipping his liqueur slowly with his red lips, in an artificially elegant voice he told his tale unconcernedly:

'They brought him to the station. His passport—Korney Sapietov, resident in Kolpin or something of the kind. Of course the devil was drunk, absolutely. "Put him into a cold cell and sober him down." General rule. That very moment I happened to drop into the inspector's office. I had a look. By Jove, an old friend: Sanka the Butcher—triple murder and sacrilege. Instantly I gave the constable on duty a wink, and went out into the corridor as though nothing had happened. The constable came out to me. "What 's the matter, Leonti Spiridonovich?" "Just send that gentleman round to the Detective Bureau for a minute." They brought him. Not a muscle in his face moved. I just looked him in the eyes and said':—Leonka rapped his knuckles meaningly on the table—'"Is it a long time, Sanka, since you left Odessa and decided to honour us here?" Of course he 's quite indifferent—playing the fool. Not a word. Oh, he 's a bright one, too. "I haven't any idea who Sanka the Butcher is. I am . . . so and so." So I come up to him, catch hold of him by the beard—hey, presto—the beard 's left in my hand. False! . . . " Will you own up now, you son of a bitch?" "I haven't any idea." Then I let fly straight at his nose—once, twice—a bloody mess. " Will you own up?" " I haven't any idea." " Ah, that 's your game, is it? I gave you a decent chance before. Now, you 've got yourself to thank. Bring Arsenti the Flea here." We had a prisoner of that name. He hated Sanka to death. Of course, my dear, I knew how they stood. They brought the Flea. " Well, Flea, who 's this gentleman?" The Flea laughs. " Why Sanka the Butcher, of course? How do you do, Sanichka? Have you been honouring us a long while? How did you get on in Odessa?" Then the Butcher gave in. " All right, Leonti Spiridonovich. I give in. Nothing can get away from you. Give us a cigarette." Of course I gave him one. I never refuse them, out of charity. The servant of God was taken away. He just looked at the Flea, no more. I thought, well, the Flea will have to pay for that. The Butcher will do him in for sure.'

'Do him in?' Genka asked with servile confidence, in a terrified whisper.

'Absolutely. Do him in. That 's the kind of man he is!'

He sipped his glass complacently. Genka looked at him with fixed, frightened eyes, so intently that her mouth even opened and watered. She smacked her hands on her lips.

'My God, how awful! Just think,

Clotilduchka! And you weren't afraid, Leonya?'

'Well, am I to be frightened of every vagabond?'

The rapt attention of the woman excited him, and he began to invent a story that students had been making bombs somewhere on Vassiliev Island, and that the Government had instructed him to arrest the conspirators. Bombs there were—it was proved afterwards—twelve thousand of them. If they 'd all exploded then not only the house they were in, but half Petersburg, perhaps, would have been blown to atoms. . . . Next came a thrilling story of Leonka's extraordinary heroism, when he disguised himself as a student, entered the 'devil's workshop,' gave a sign to some one outside the window, and disarmed the villains in a second. He caught one of them by the sleeve at the very moment when he was going to explode a lot of bombs.

Genka groaned, was terror-stricken, slapped her legs, and continually turned to Clotilde with exclamations:

'Ah! what do you think of all that? Just think what scoundrels these students are, Clotilduchka! I never liked them.'

At last, stirred to her very depths by her lover, she hung on his neck and began to kiss him loudly.

'Leonichka, my darling! It 's terrible to listen to, even! And you aren't frightened of anything!'

He complacently twisted his left moustache upwards, and let drop carelessly: 'Why be afraid? You can only die once. That's what I'm paid for.'

Clotilde was tormented all the while by jealous envy of her friend's magnificent lover. She vaguely suspected that there was a great deal of lying in Leonka's stories; while she now had something utterly extraordinary in her hands, such as no one had ever had before, something that would immediately take all the shine out of Leonka's exploits. For some minutes she hesitated. A faint echo of the tender pity for Ribnikov still restrained her. But a hysterical yearning to shine took hold of her, and she said in a dull, quiet voice: 'Do you know what I wanted to tell you, Leonya? I've got such a queer visitor to-day.'

'H'm. You think he's a sharper?' he asked condescendingly. Genka was offended.

'A sharper, you say! That's your story. Some drunken officer.'

'No, you mustn't say that,' Leonka pompously interrupted. 'It happens that sharpers get themselves up as officers. What was it you were going to say, Clotilde?'

Then she told the story of Ribnikov with every detail, displaying a petty and utterly feminine talent for observation: she told how they called him General Kuroki, his Japanese face, his strange tenderness and passion, his delirium, and finally now he said 'Banzai!'

'You 're not lying?' Leonka said quickly. Keen points of fire lit in his eyes.

'I swear it 's true! May I be rooted to the ground if it 's a lie! You look through the keyhole, I 'll go in and open the shutter. He 's as like a Japanese as two peas.'

Leonka rose. Without haste, with a serious look, he put on his overcoat, carefully feeling his left inside pocket.

'Come on,' he said resolutely. 'Who did he arrive with?'

Only Karyukov and Strahlmann remained of the all-night party. Karyukov could not be awakened, and Strahlmaun muttered something indistinctly. He was still half drunk and his eyes were heavy and red.

'What officer? Blast him to hell! He came up to us when we were in the "Buff," but where he came from nobody knows.'

He began to dress immediately, snorting angrily. Leonka apologised and went out. He had already managed to get a glimpse of Ribnikov's face through the keyhole, and through he had some doubts remaining, he was a good patriot, distinguished for impertinence and not devoid of imagination. He decided to act on his own responsibility. In a moment he was on the balcony whistling for help.

VII

Ribnikov woke suddenly as though an imperative voice within him had said 'Wake up.' An hour and a half of sleep had completely refreshed him. First of all he stared suspiciously at the door: it seemed to him that some one was watching him from there with a fixed stare. Then he looked round. The shutter was half open so that every little thing in the room could be seen. The woman was sitting by the table opposite the bed, silent and pale, regarding him with big, bright eyes.

'What's happened?' Ribnikov asked in alarm. 'Tell me, what's been happening here?'

She did not answer, but her chin began to tremble and her teeth chattered.

A suspicious, cruel light came into the officer's eyes. He bent his whole body from the bed with his ear to the door. The noise of many feet, of men evidently unused to moving cautiously, approached along the corridor, and suddenly was quiet before the door.

Ribnikov with a quick, soft movement leapt from the bed and twice turned the key. There was an instant knock at the door. With a cry the woman turned her face to the table and buried her head in her hands.

In a few seconds the captain was dressed. Again they knocked at the door. He had only his cap with him; he had left his sword and overcoat below. He was pale but perfectly calm. Even his hands did not tremble while he dressed himself, and all his movements were quite unhurried and adroit. Doing up the last button of his tunic, he went over to the woman, and suddenly squeezed her arm above the wrist with such terrible strength that her face purpled with the blood that rushed to her head.

'You!' he said quietly, in an angry whisper, without moving his jaws. 'If you move or make a sound, I'll kill you. . . .'

Again they knocked at the door, and a dull voice came: 'Open the door, if you please.'

The captain now no longer limped. Quickly and silently he ran to the window, jumped on to the window-ledge with the soft spring of a cat, opened the shutters and with one sweep flung wide the window frames. Below him the paved yard showed white with scanty grass between the stones, and the branches of a few thin trees pointed upwards. He did not hesitate for a second; but at the very moment that he sat sideways on the iron frame of the window-sill, resting on it with his left hand, with one foot already hanging down, and prepared to leap with his whole body, the woman threw herself upon him with a piercing cry and caught him by the left arm. Tearing himself away, he made a false movement and suddenly, with a faint cry as though of surprise, fell in an awkward heap straight down on the stones.

Almost at the very second the old door fell flat into the room. First Leonka ran in, out of breath, showing his teeth; his eyes were aflame. After him came huge policemen, stamping and holding their swords in their left hands. When he saw the open window and the woman holding on the frame and screaming without pause, Leonka quickly understood what had happened. He was really a brave man, and without a thought or a word, as though he had already planned it, he took a running leap through the window.

He landed two steps away from Ribnikov, who lay motionless on his side. In spite of the drumming in his head, and the intense pain in his belly and his heels from the fall, he kept his head, and instantly threw himself heavily with the full weight of his body on the captain.

'A-ah. I've got you now,' he uttered hoarsely, crushing his victim in mad exasperation.

The captain did not resist. His eyes burned with an implacable hatred. But he was pale as death, and a pink froth stood in bubbles on his lips.

'Don't crush me,' he whispered. 'My leg's broken.'

III

THE OUTRAGE

THE OUTRAGE

A TRUE STORY

It was five o'clock on a July afternoon. The heat was terrible. The whole of the huge stone-built town breathed out heat like a glowing furnace. The glare of the white-walled house was insufferable. The asphalt pavements grew soft and burned the feet. The shadows of the acacias spread over the cobbled road, pitiful and weary. They too seemed hot. The sea, pale in the sunlight, lay heavy and immobile as one dead. Over the streets hung a white dust.

In the foyer of one of the private theatres a small committee of local barristers who had undertaken to conduct the cases of those who had suffered in the last pogrom against the Jews was reaching the end of its daily task. There were nineteen of them, all juniors, young, progressive and conscientious men. The sitting was without formality, and white ducks, flannels and white alpaca were in the majority. They sat anywhere, at little marble tables, and the chairman stood in front of an empty counter where chocolates were sold in the winter.

The barristers were quite exhausted by the heat which poured in through the windows, with the dazzling sunlight and the noise of the streets.

The proceedings went lazily and with a certain irritation.

A tall young man with a fair moustache and thin hair was in the chair. He was dreaming voluptuously how he would be off in an instant on his new-bought bicycle to the bungalow. He would undress quickly, and without waiting to cool, still bathed in sweat, would fling himself into the clear, cold, sweet-smelling sea. His whole body was enervated and tense, thrilled by the thought. Impatiently moving the papers before him, he spoke in a drowsy voice.

'So, Joseph Moritzovich will conduct the case of Rubinchik. . . . Perhaps there is still a statement to be made on the order of the day ?'

His youngest colleague, a short, stout Karaim, very black and lively, said in a whisper so that every one could hear : 'On the order of the day, the best thing would be iced *kvass*. . . .'

The chairman gave him a stern side-glance, but could not restrain a smile. He sighed and put both his hands on the table to raise himself and declare the meeting closed, when the door-keeper, who stood at the entrance to the theatre, suddenly moved forward and said : 'There are seven people outside, sir. They want to come in.'

The chairman looked impatiently round the company.

'What is to be done, gentlemen ?'

Voices were heard.

'Next time. *Basta !*'

‘ Let ’em put it in writing.’

‘ If they ’ll get it over quickly. . . . Decide it at once.’

‘ Let ’em go to the devil. Phew ! It ’s like boiling pitch.’

‘ Let them in.’ The chairman gave a sign with his head, annoyed. ‘ Then bring me a Vichy, please. But it must be cold.’

The porter opened the door and called down the corridor : ‘ Come in. They say you may.’

Then seven of the most surprising and unexpected individuals filed into the foyer. First appeared a full-grown, confident man in a smart suit, of the colour of dry sea-sand, in a magnificent pink shirt with white stripes and a crimson rose in his buttonhole. From the front his head looked like an upright bean, from the side like a horizontal bean. His face was adorned with a strong, bushy, martial moustache. He wore dark blue pince-nez on his nose, on his hands straw-coloured gloves. In his left hand he held a black walking-stick with a silver mount, in his right a light blue handkerchief.

The other six produced a strange, chaotic, incongruous impression, exactly as though they had all hastily pooled not merely their clothes, but their hands, feet and heads as well. There was a man with the splendid profile of a Roman senator, dressed in rags and tatters. Another wore an elegant dress waistcoat, from the deep opening of which a dirty little-Russian shirt leapt to the eye. Here were the unbalanced faces of the criminal type, but looking with a confidence that nothing could shake. All these men, in spite of their apparent youth, evidently possessed a large experience of life, an easy manner, a bold approach, and some hidden, suspicious cunning.

The gentleman in the sandy suit bowed just his head, neatly and easily, and said with a half-question in his voice : 'Mr. Chairman ?'

'Yes. I am the chairman,' said the latter. 'What is your business ?'

'We—all whom you see before you,' the gentleman began in a quiet voice and turned round to indicate his companions, 'we come as delegates from the United Rostov-Kharkov-and-Odessa-Nicolaiev Association of Thieves.'

The barristers began to shift in their seats.

The chairman flung himself back and opened his eyes wide. 'Association of *what* ?' he said, perplexed.

'The Association of Thieves,' the gentleman in the sandy suit coolly repeated. 'As for myself, my comrades did me the signal honour of electing me as the spokesman of the deputation.'

'Very . . . pleased,' the chairman said uncertainly.

'Thank you. All seven of us are ordinary thieves—naturally of different departments. The Association has authorised us to put before your esteemed Committee'—the gentleman again made an elegant bow—'our respectful demand for assistance.'

'I don't quite understand . . . quite frankly . . . what is the connection. . . .' The chairman waved his hands helplessly. 'However, please go on.'

'The matter about which we have the courage and the honour to apply to you, gentlemen, is very clear, very simple, and very brief. It will take only six or seven minutes. I consider it my duty to warn you of this beforehand, in view of the late hour and the 115 degrees that Fahrenheit marks in the shade.' The orator expectorated slightly and glanced at his superb gold watch. 'You see, in the reports that have lately appeared in the local papers of the melancholy and terrible days of the last pogrom, there have very often been indications that among the instigators of the pogrom who were paid and organised by the police—the dregs of society, consisting of drunkards, tramps, souteneurs, and hooligans from the slums—thieves were also to be found. At first we were silent, but finally we considered ourselves under the necessity of protesting against such an unjust and serious accusation, before the face of the whole of intellectual society. I know well that in the eye of the law we are offenders and enemies of society. But imagine only for a moment, gentlemen, the situation of this enemy of society when he is accused wholesale of an offence which he not only never committed, but which he is ready to resist with the whole strength of his soul. It goes without saying that he will feel the outrage of such an injustice more keenly than a normal, average, fortunate citizen. Now, we declare that the accusation brought against us is utterly devoid of all basis, not merely of fact but even of logic. I intend to prove this in a few words if the honourable committee will kindly listen.'

'Proceed,' said the chairman.

'Please do . . . Please . . .' was heard from the barristers, now animated.

'I offer you my sincere thanks in the name of all my comrades. Believe me, you will never repent your attention to the representatives of our . . . well, let us say, slippery, but nevertheless difficult, profession. "So we begin," as Giraldoni sings in the prologue to *Pagliacci*.

'But first I would ask your permission, Mr. Chairman, to quench my thirst a little. . . . Porter, bring me a lemonade and a glass of English bitter, there 's a good fellow. Gentlemen, I will not speak of the moral aspect of our profession nor of its social importance. Doubtless you know better than I the striking and brilliant paradox of Proudhon: *La propriété c'est le vol*—a paradox if you like, but one that has never yet been refuted by the sermons of cowardly bourgeois or fat priests. For instance: a father accumulates a million by energetic and clever exploitation, and leaves to his son—a rickety, lazy, ignorant, degenerate idiot, a brainless maggot, a true parasite. Potentially a million roubles is a million working days, the absolutely irrational right to labour, sweat, life, and blood of a terrible number of men. Why? What is the ground or reason? Utterly unknown. Then why not agree with the proposition, gentlemen, that our profession is to some extent as it were a correction of the excessive accumulation of values in the hands of individuals, and serves as a protest against all the hardships, abominations, arbitrariness, violence, and negligence of the human personality, against all the monstrosities created by the bourgeois capitalistic organisation of modern society? Sooner or later, this order of things will assuredly be overturned by the social revolution. Property will pass away into the limbo of melancholy memories and with it, alas! we will disappear from the face of the earth, we, *les braves chevaliers d'industrie.*'

The orator paused to take the tray from the hands of the porter, and placed it near to his hand on the table.

'Excuse me, gentlemen. . . . Here, my good man, take this . . . and by the way, when you go out shut the door close behind you.'

'Very good, your Excellency!' the porter bawled in jest.

The orator drank off half a glass and continued: 'However, let us leave aside the philosophical, social, and economic aspects of the question. I do not wish to fatigue your attention. I must nevertheless point out that our profession very closely approaches the idea of that which is called art. Into it enter all the elements which go to form art—vocation, inspiration, fantasy, inventiveness, ambition, and a long and arduous apprenticeship to the science. From it is absent virtue alone, concerning which the great

Karamzin wrote with such stupendous and fiery fascination. Gentlemen, nothing is further from my intention than to trifle with you and waste your precious time with idle paradoxes; but I cannot avoid expounding my idea briefly. To an outsider's ear it sounds absurdly wild and ridiculous to speak of the vocation of a thief. However, I venture to assure you that this vocation is a reality. There are men who possess a peculiarly strong visual memory, sharpness and accuracy of eye, presence of mind, dexterity of hand, and above all a subtle sense of touch, who are as it were born into God's world for the sole and special purpose of becoming distinguished card-sharpers. The pickpockets' profession demands extraordinary nimbleness and agility, a terrific certainty of movement, not to mention a ready wit, a talent for observation and strained attention. Some have a positive vocation for breaking open safes: from their tenderest childhood they are attracted by the mysteries of every kind of complicated mechanism — bicycles, sewing machines, clock-work toys and watches. Finally, gentlemen, there are people with an hereditary animus against private property. You may call this phenomenon degeneracy. But I tell you that you cannot entice a true thief, and thief by vocation, into the prose of honest vegetation by any gingerbread reward, or by the offer of a secure position, or by the gift of money, or by a woman's love: because there is here a permanent beauty of risk, a fascinating abyss of danger, the delightful sinking of the heart, the impetuous pulsation of life, the ecstasy! You are armed with the protection of the law, by locks, revolvers, telephones, police and soldiery; but we only by our own dexterity, cunning and fearlessness. We are the foxes, and society—is a chicken-run guarded by dogs. Are you aware that the most artistic and gifted natures in our villages become horse-thieves and poachers? What would you have? Life has been so meagre, so insipid, so intolerably dull to eager and high-spirited souls!

'I pass on to inspiration. Gentlemen, doubtless you have had to read of thefts that were supernatural in design and execution. In the headlines of the newspapers they are called "An Amazing Robbery," or "An Ingenious Swindle," or again "A Clever Ruse of the Mobsmen." In such cases our bourgeois paterfamilias waves his hands and exclaims: "What a terrible thing! If only their abilities were turned to good—their inventiveness, their amazing knowledge of human psychology, their self-possession, their fearlessness, their incomparable histrionic powers! What extraordinary benefits they would bring to the country!" But it is well known that the bourgeois paterfamilias was specially devised by Heaven to utter commonplaces and trivialities. I myself sometimes—we thieves are sentimental people, I confess—I myself sometimes admire a beautiful sunset in Alexandra Park or by the sea-shore. And I am always certain beforehand that some one near me will say with infallible *aplomb*: "Look at it. If it were put into a picture no one would ever believe it!" I turn round and naturally I see a self-satisfied, full-fed paterfamilias, who delights in repeating some one else's silly statement as though it were his own. As for our dear country, the bourgeois paterfamilias looks upon it as though it were a roast turkey. If you 've managed to cut the best part of the bird for yourself, eat it quietly in a comfortable corner and praise God. But he 's not really the important person. I was led away by my detestation of vulgarity and I apologise for the digression. The real point is that genius and inspiration, even when they are not devoted to the service of the Orthodox Church, remain rare and beautiful things. Progress is a law—and theft too has its creation.

'Finally, our profession is by no means as easy and pleasant as it seems to the first glance. It demands long experience, constant practice, slow and painful apprenticeship. It comprises in itself hundreds of supple, skilful processes that the cleverest juggler cannot compass. That I may not give you only empty words, gentlemen, I will perform a few experiments before you, now. I ask you to have every confidence in the demonstrators. We are all at present in the enjoyment of legal freedom, and though we are usually watched, and every one of us is known by face, and our photographs adorn the albums of all detective departments, for the time being we are not under the necessity of hiding ourselves from anybody. If any one of you should recognise any of us in the future under different circumstances, we ask you earnestly always to act in accordance with your professional duties and your obligations as citizens. In grateful return for your kind attention we have decided to declare your property inviolable, and to invest it with a thieves' taboo. However, I proceed to business.'

The orator turned round and gave an order: 'Sesoi the Great, will you come this way!'

An enormous fellow with a stoop, whose hands reached to his knees, without a forehead or a neck, like a big, fair Hercules, came forward. He grinned stupidly and rubbed his left eyebrow in his confusion.

'Can't do nothin' here,' he said hoarsely.

The gentleman in the sandy suit spoke for him, turning to the committee.

'Gentlemen, before you stands a respected member of our association. His speciality is breaking open safes, iron strong boxes, and other receptacles for monetary tokens. In his night work he sometimes avails himself of the electric current of the lighting installation for fusing metals. Unfortunately he has nothing on which he can demonstrate the best items of his repertoire. He will open the most elaborate lock irreproachably. . . . By the way, this door here, it 's locked, is it not?'

Every one turned to look at the door, on which a printed notice hung: 'Stage Door. Strictly Private.'

'Yes, the door 's locked, evidently,' the chairman agreed.

'Admirable. Sesoi the Great, will you be so kind?'

''Tain't nothin' at all,' said the giant leisurely.

He went close to the door, shook it cautiously with his hand, took out of his pocket a small bright instrument, bent down to the keyhole, made some almost imperceptible movements with the tool, suddenly straightened and flung the door wide in silence. The chairman had his watch in his hands. The whole affair took only ten seconds.

'Thank you, Sesoi the Great,' said the gentleman in the sandy suit politely. 'You may go back to your seat.'

But the chairman interrupted in some alarm: 'Excuse me. This is all very interesting and instructive, but . . . is it included in your esteemed colleague's profession to be able to lock the door again?'

'Ah, *mille pardons*.' The gentleman bowed hurriedly. 'It slipped my mind. Sesoi the Great, would you oblige?'

The door was locked with the same adroitness and the same silence. The esteemed colleague waddled back to his friends, grinning.

'Now I will have the honour to show you the skill of one of our comrades who is in the line of picking pockets in theatres and railway-stations,' continued the orator. 'He is still very young, but you may to some extent judge from the delicacy of his present work of the heights he will attain by diligence. Yasha ! ' A swarthy youth in a blue silk blouse and long glacé boots, like a gipsy, came forward with a swagger, fingering the tassels of his belt, and merrily screwing up his big, impudent black eyes with yellow whites.

'Gentlemen,' said the gentleman in the sandy suit persuasively, 'I must ask if one of you would be kind enough to submit himself to a little experiment. I assure you this will be an exhibition only, just a game.'

He looked round over the seated company.

The short plump Karaim, black as a beetle, came forward from his table.

'At your service,' he said amusingly.

'Yasha ! ' The orator signed with his head.

Yasha came close to the solicitor. On his left arm, which was bent, hung a bright-coloured, figured scarf.

'Suppose yer in church, or at a bar in one of the 'alls,—or watchin' a circus,' he began in a sugary, fluent voice. 'I see straight off—there 's a toff. . . . Excuse me, sir. Suppose you 're the toff. There 's no offence—just means a rich gent, decent enough, but don't know his way about. First—what 's he likely to 'ave about 'im ? All sorts. Mostly, a ticker and a chain. Whereabouts does 'e keep 'em. Somewhere in 'is top weskit pocket— 'ere. Others 'ave 'em in the bottom pocket. Just 'ere. Purse—most always in the trousers, except when a greeny keeps it in 'is jacket. Cigar-case. 'Ave a look first what it is—gold, silver—with a monogram. Leather—wot decent man 'd soil 'is 'ands? Cigar-case. Seven pockets: 'ere, 'ere 'ere, up there, there, 'ere and 'ere again. That 's right, ain't it? That 's 'ow you go to work.'

As he spoke the young man smiled. His eyes shone straight into the barrister's. With a quick, dexterous movement of his right hand he pointed to various portions of his clothes.

'Then agen you might see a pin 'ere in the tie. 'Owever we do not appropriate. Such *gents* nowadays—they 'ardly ever wear a reel stone. Then I comes up to 'im. I begin straight off to talk to 'im like a gent: "Sir, would you be so kind as to give me a light from your cigarette"—or something of the sort. At any rate, I enter into conversation. Wot 's next? I look 'im straight in the peepers, just like this. Only two of me fingers are at it—just this and this.' Yasha lifted two fingers of his right hand on a level with the solicitor's face, the forefinger and the middle finger and moved them about.

'D' you see? With these two fingers I run over the 'ole pianner. Nothin' wonderful in it: one, two, three—ready. Any man who wasn't stupid could learn easily. That 's all it is. Most ordinary business. I thank you.'

The pickpocket swung on his heel as if to return to his seat.

'Yasha!' The gentleman in the sandy suit said with meaning weight. 'Yasha!' he repeated sternly.

Yasha stopped. His back was turned to the

barrister, but he evidently gave his representative an imploring look, because the latter frowned and shook his head.

'Yasha!' he said for the third time, in a threatening tone.

'Huh!' The young thief grunted in vexation and turned to face the solicitor. 'Where 's your little watch, sir?' he said in a piping voice.

'Ach,' the Karaim brought himself up sharp.

'You see—now you say "Ach,"' Yasha continued reproachfully. 'All the while you were admiring me right 'and, I was operatin' yer watch with my left. Just with these two little fingers, under the scarf. That 's why we carry a scarf. Since your chain 's not worth anything—a present from some *mamselle* and the watch is a gold one, I 've left you the chain as a keepsake. Take it,' he added with a sigh, holding out the watch.

'But . . . That is clever,' the barrister said in confusion. 'I didn't notice it at all.'

'That 's our business,' Yasha said with pride.

He swaggered back to his comrades. Meantime the orator took a drink from his glass and continued.

'Now, gentlemen, our next collaborator will give you an exhibition of some ordinary card tricks, which are worked at fairs, on steamboats and railways. With three cards, for instance, an ace, a queen, and a six, he can quite easily. . . . But perhaps you are tired of these demonstrations, gentlemen.' . . .

'Not at all. It 's extremely interesting,' the

chairman answered affably. 'I should like to ask one question—that is if it is not too indiscreet—what is your own speciality ?'

'Mine . . . H'm. . . . No, how could it be an indiscretion ? . . . I work the big diamond shops . . . and my other business is banks,' answered the orator with a modest smile. 'Don't think this occupation is easier than others. Enough that I know four European languages, German, French, English, and Italian, without speaking of Polish, Ukrainian and Yiddish. But shall I show you some more experiments, Mr. Chairman ?'

The chairman looked at his watch.

'Unfortunately the time is too short,' he said. 'Wouldn't it be better to pass on to the substance of your business ? Besides the experiments we have just seen have amply convinced us of the talent of your esteemed associates. . . . Am I not right, Isaac Abramovich ?'

'Yes, yes . . . absolutely,' the Karaim barrister readily confirmed.

'Admirable,' the gentleman in the sandy suit kindly agreed. 'My dear Count'—he turned to a blonde, curly-haired man, with a face like a billiard-maker on a bank-holiday—'put your instruments away. They will not be wanted. I have only a few words more to say, gentlemen. Now that you have convinced yourselves that our art, although it does not enjoy the patronage of high-placed individuals, is nevertheless an art; and you have probably come to my opinion that this art is one which demands many personal qualities besides constant labour, danger, and unpleasant misunderstandings—you will also, I hope, believe that it is possible to become attached to its practice and to love and esteem it, however strange that may appear at first sight. Picture to yourselves that a famous poet of talent, whose tales and poems adorn the pages of our best magazines, is suddenly offered the chance of writing verses at a penny a line, signed into the bargain, as an advertisement for "Cigarettes Jasmine"—or that a slander was spread about one of you distinguished barristers, accusing him of making a business of concocting evidence for divorce cases, or of writing petitions from the cabmen to the governor in public-houses! Certainly your relatives, friends and acquaintances wouldn't believe it. But the rumour has already done its poisonous work, and you have to live through minutes of torture. Now picture to yourselves that such a disgraceful and vexatious slander, started by God knows whom, begins to threaten not only your good name and your quiet digestion, but your freedom, your health, and even your life!

'This is the position of us thieves, now being slandered by the newspapers. I must explain. There is in existence a class of scum—*passez-moi le mot*—whom we call their "Mothers' Darlings." With these we are unfortunately confused. They have neither shame nor conscience, a dissipated riff-raff, mothers' useless darlings, idle, clumsy drones, shop assistants who commit unskilful thefts. He thinks nothing of living on his mistress, a prostitute, like the male mackerel, who always swims after the female and lives on her excrements. He is capable of robbing a child with violence in a dark alley, in order to get a penny: he will kill a man in his sleep and torture an old woman. These men are the pests of our profession. For them the beauties and the traditions of the art have no existence. They watch us real, talented thieves like a pack of jackals after a lion. Suppose I 've managed to bring off an important job—we won't mention the fact that I have to leave two-thirds of what I get to the receivers who sell the goods and discount the notes, or the customary subsidies to our incorruptible police—I still have to share out something to each one of these parasites, who have got wind of my job, by accident, hearsay, or a casual glance.

'So we call them *Motients*, which means "half," a corruption of *moitié*. . . . Original etymology. I pay him only because he knows and may inform against me. And it mostly happens that even when he 's got his share he runs off to the police in order to get another half-sovereign. We, honest thieves. . . . Yes, you may laugh, gentlemen, but I repeat it: we honest thieves detest these reptiles. We have another name for them, a stigma of ignominy; but I dare not utter it here out of respect for the place and for my audience. Oh, yes, they would gladly accept an invitation to a pogrom. The thought that we may be confused with them is a hundred times more insulting to us even than the accusation of taking part in a pogrom.

'Gentlemen! While I have been speaking, I have often noticed smiles on your faces. I understand you: our presence here, our application for your assistance, and above all the unexpectedness of such a phenomenon as a systematic organisation of thieves, with delegates who are thieves, and a leader of the deputation, also a thief by profession—it is all so original that it must inevitably arouse a smile. But now I will speak from the depth of my heart. Let us be rid of our outward wrappings, gentlemen, let us speak as men to men.

'Almost all of us are educated, and all love books. We don't only read the adventures of Roqueambole, as the realistic writers say of us. Do you think our hearts did not bleed and our cheeks did not burn from shame, as though we had been slapped in the face, all the time that this unfortunate, disgraceful, accursed, cowardly war lasted. Do you really think that our souls do not flame with anger when our country is lashed with Cossack-whips, and trodden underfoot, shot and spit at by mad, exasperated men? Will you not believe that we thieves meet every step towards the liberation to come with a thrill of ecstasy?

'We understand, every one of us—perhaps only a little less than you barristers, gentlemen—the real sense of the pogroms. Every time that some dastardly event or some ignominious failure has occurred, after executing a martyr in a dark corner of a fortress, or after deceiving public confidence, some one who is hidden and unapproachable gets frightened of the people's anger and diverts its vicious element upon the heads of innocent Jews. Whose diabolical mind invents these pogroms—these titanic blood-lettings, these cannibal amusements for the dark, bestial souls?

'We all see with certain clearness that the last convulsions of the bureaucracy are at hand. Forgive me if I present it imaginatively. There was a people that had a chief temple, wherein dwelt a bloodthirsty deity, behind a curtain, guarded by priests. Once fearless hands tore the curtain away. Then all the people saw, instead of a god, a huge, shaggy, voracious spider, like a loathsome cuttlefish. They beat it and shoot at it: it is dismembered already; but still in the frenzy of its final agony it stretches over all the ancient temple its disgusting, clawing tentacles. And the priests, themselves under sentence of death, push into the monster's grasp all whom they can seize in their terrified, trembling fingers.

'Forgive me. What I have said is probably wild and incoherent. But I am somewhat agitated. Forgive me. I continue. We thieves by profession know better than any one else how these pogroms were organised. We wander everywhere: into public houses, markets, teashops, doss-houses, public places, the harbour. We can swear before God and man and posterity that we have seen how the police organise the massacres, without shame and almost without concealment. We know them all by face, in uniform or disguise. They invited many of us to take part; but there was none so vile among us as to give even the outward consent that fear might have extorted.

'You know, of course, how the various strata of Russian society behave towards the police? It is not even respected by those who avail themselves of its dark services. But we despise and hate it three, ten times more—not because many of us have been tortured in the detective departments, which are just chambers of horror, beaten almost to death, beaten with whips of ox-hide and of rubber in order to extort a confession or to make us betray a comrade. Yes, we hate them for that too. But we thieves, all of us who have been in prison, have a mad passion for freedom. Therefore we despise our gaolers with all the hatred that a human heart can feel. I will speak for myself. I have been tortured three times by police detectives till I was half dead. My lungs and liver have been shattered. In the mornings I spit blood until I can breathe no more. But if I were told that I will be spared a fourth flogging only by shaking hands with a chief of the detective police, I would refuse to do it!

'And then the newspapers say that we took from these hands Judas-money, dripping with human blood. No, gentlemen, it is a slander which stabs our very soul, and inflicts insufferable pain. Not money, nor threats, nor promises will suffice to make us mercenary murderers of our brethren, nor accomplices with them.'

'Never . . . No . . . No . . ,' his comrades standing behind him began to murmur.

'I will say more,' the thief continued. 'Many of us protected the victims during this pogrom. Our friend, called Sesoi the Great—you have just seen him, gentlemen—was then lodging with a Jewish braid-maker on the Moldavanka. With a poker in his hands he defended his landlord from a great horde of assassins. It is true, Sesoi the Great is a man of enormous physical strength, and this is well known to many of the inhabitants of the Moldavanka. But you must agree, gentlemen, that in these moments Sesoi the Great looked straight into the face of death. Our comrade Martin the Miner—this gentleman here'—the orator pointed to a pale, bearded man with beautiful eyes who was holding himself in the background—'saved an old Jewess, whom he had never seen before, who was being pursued by a crowd of these *canaille*. They broke his head with a crowbar for his pains, smashed his arm in two places and splintered a rib. He is only just out of hospital. That is the way our most ardent and determined members acted. The others trembled for anger and wept for their own impotence.

'None of us will forget the horrors of those bloody days and bloody nights lit up by the glare of fires, those sobbing women, those little children's bodies torn to pieces and left lying in the street. But for all that not one of us thinks that the police and the mob are the real origin of the evil. These tiny, stupid. loathsome vermin are only a senseless fist that is governed by a vile, calculating mind, moved by a diabolical will.

'Yes, gentlemen,' the orator continued, 'we thieves have nevertheless merited your legal contempt. But when you, noble gentlemen, need the help of clever, brave, obedient men at the barricades, men who will be ready to meet death with a song and a jest on their lips for the most glorious word in the world—Freedom—will you cast us off then and order us away because of an inveterate revulsion? Damn it all, the first victim in the French Revolution was a prostitute. She jumped up on to a barricade, with her skirt caught elegantly up into her hand and called out: "Which of you soldiers will dare to shoot a woman?" Yes, by God.' The orator exclaimed aloud and brought down his fist on to the marble table top: 'They killed her, but her action was magnificent, and the beauty of her words immortal.

'If you should drive us away on the great day, we will turn to you and say: "You spotless Cherubim—if human thoughts had the power to wound, kill, and rob man of honour and property, then which of you innocent doves would not deserve the knout and imprisonment for life?" Then we will go away from you and build our own gay, sporting, desperate thieves' barricade, and will die with such united songs on our lips that you will envy us, you who are whiter than snow!

'But I have been once more carried away. Forgive me. I am at the end. You now see, gentlemen, what feelings the newspaper slanders have excited in us. Believe in our sincerity and do what you can to remove the filthy stain which has so unjustly been cast upon us. I have finished.'

He went away from the table and joined his comrades. The barristers were whispering in an undertone, very much as the magistrates of the bench at sessions. Then the chairman rose.

'We trust you absolutely, and we will make every effort to clear your association of this most grievous charge. At the same time my colleagues have authorised me, gentlemen, to convey to you their deep respect for your passionate feelings as citizens. And for my own part I ask the leader of the deputation for permission to shake him by the hand.'

The two men, both tall and serious, held each other's hands in a strong, masculine grip.

The barristers were leaving the theatre: but four of them hung back a little by the clothes peg in the hall. Isaac Abramovich could not find his new, smart grey hat anywhere. In its place on the wooden peg hung a cloth cap jauntily flattened in on either side.

'Yasha!' The stern voice of the orator was suddenly heard from the other side of the door. 'Yasha! It's the last time I'll speak to you, curse you! . . . Do you hear?'

The heavy door opened wide. The gentleman

in the sandy suit entered. In his hands he held Isaac Abramovich's hat; on his face was a well-bred smile.

'Gentlemen, for Heaven's sake forgive us—an odd little misunderstanding. One of our comrades exchanged his hat quite by accident. . . . Oh, it is yours! A thousand pardons. Doorkeeper! Why don't you keep an eye on things, my good fellow, eh? Just give me that cap, there. Once more, I ask you to forgive me, gentlemen.'

With a pleasant bow and the same well-bred smile he made his way quickly into the street.

IV
THE WITCH

THE WITCH

(OLYESSIA)

I

YARMOLA the gamekeeper, my servant, cook, and fellow-hunter, entered the room with a load of wood on his shoulder, threw it heavily on the floor, and blew on his frozen fingers.

'What a wind there is outside, sir,' he said, squatting on his heels in front of the oven door. 'We must make a good fire in the stove. Will you give me a match, please ?'

'It means we shan't have a chance at the hares to-morrow, eh ? What do you think, Yarmola ?'

'No. . . . Out of the question. . . . Do you hear the snowstorm ? The hares lie still—no sound. . . . You won't see a single track to-morrow.'

Fate had thrown me for a whole six months into a dull little village in Volhymnia, on the border of Polyessie, and hunting was my sole occupation and delight. I confess that at the time when the business in the village was offered me, I had no idea that I should feel so intolerably dull. I went even with joy. 'Polyessie . . . a remote place . . . the bosom of Nature . . . simple ways . . . primitive natures,' I thought as I sat in the railway carriage, 'completely unfamiliar people, with strange customs and a curious language . . . and there are sure to be thousands of romantic legends, traditions, and songs!' At that time—since I have to confess, I may as well confess everything—I had already published a story with two murders and one suicide in an unknown newspaper, and I knew theoretically that it was useful for writers to observe customs.

But—either the peasants of Perebrod were distinguished by a particularly obstinate uncommunicativeness, or I myself did not know how to approach them—my relations with them went no further than that when they saw me a mile off they took off their caps, and when they came alongside said sternly, 'God with you,' which should mean 'God help you.' And when I attempted to enter into conversation with them they looked at me in bewilderment, refused to understand the simplest questions, and tried all the while to kiss my hands—a habit that has survived from their Polish serfdom.

I read all the books I had with me very soon. Out of boredom—though at first it seemed to me very unpleasant—I made an attempt to get to know the local 'intellectuals,' a Catholic priest who lived fifteen versts away, the gentleman organist who lived with him, the local police-sergeant, and the bailiff of the neighbouring estate, a retired non-commissioned officer. But nothing came of it.

Then I tried to occupy myself with doctoring

the inhabitants of Perebrod. I had at my disposal castor-oil, carbolic acid, boracic, and iodine. But here, besides the scantiness of my knowledge, I came up against the complete impossibility of making a diagnosis, because the symptoms of all patients were exactly the same: 'I 've got a pain inside,' and 'I can't take bite nor sup.'

For instance an old woman comes to me. With a disturbed look she wipes her nose with the forefinger of her right hand. I catch a glimpse of her brown skin as she takes a couple of eggs from her bosom, and puts them on the table. Then she begins to seize my hands in order to plant a kiss on them. I hide them and persuade the old woman: 'Come, granny . . . don't. . . . I 'm not a priest . . . I have no right. . . . What 's the matter with you?'

'I 've got a pain in the inside, sir; just right inside, so that I can't take nor bite nor sup.'

'Have you had it long?'

'How do I know?' she answers with a question. 'It just burns, burns all the while. Not a bite, nor a sup.'

However much I try, I can get no more definite symptoms.

'Don't you worry,' the non.-com. bailiff once said to me. 'They 'll cure themselves. It 'll dry on them like a dog. I beg you to note I use only one medicine—sal-volatile. A peasant comes to me. "What 's the matter?" "I'm ill," says he. I just run off for the bottle of sal-volatile. "Sniff!" . . . he sniffs. . . . "Sniff again . . . go on!" He sniffs again. "Feel better?" "I do seem to feel better." "Well, then, be off, and God be with you."'

Besides I did not at all like the kissing of my hands. (Some just fell at my feet and did all they could to kiss my boots.) For it wasn't by any means the emotion of a grateful heart, but simply a loathsome habit, rooted in them by centuries of slavery and brutality. And I could only wonder at the non.-com. bailiff and the police-sergeant when I saw the imperturbable gravity with which they shoved their enormous red hands to the peasants' lips. . . .

Only hunting was left. But with the end of January came such terrible weather that even hunting was impossible. Every day there was an awful wind, and during the night a hard icy crust formed on the snow, on which the hares could run without leaving a trace. As I sat shut up in the house listening to the howling wind, I felt terribly sad, and I eagerly seized such an innocent distraction as teaching Yarmola the gamekeeper to read and write.

It came about quite curiously. Once I was writing a letter, when suddenly I felt that some one was behind me. Turning round I saw Yarmola, who had approached noiselessly, as his habit was, in his soft bast shoes.

'What d' you want, Yarmola?' I asked.

'I was only looking how you write. I wish I could. . . . No, no . . . not like you,' he began hastily, seeing me smile. 'I only wish I could write my name.'

'Why do you want to do that?' I was surprised. (It must be remembered that Yarmola is supposed to be the poorest and laziest peasant in the whole of Perebrod. His wages and earnings go in drink. There isn't such another scarecrow even among the local oxen. I thought that he would have been the last person to find reading and writing necessary.) I asked him again, doubtfully:

'What do you want to know how to write your name for?'

'You see how it stands, sir.' Yarmola answered with extraordinary softness. 'There isn't a single man who can read and write in the village. When there's a paper to be signed or some business to be done on the council or anything . . . nobody can. . . . The mayor only puts the seal; but he doesn't know what's in the paper. It would be a good thing for everybody if one of us could write his name.'

Yarmola's solicitude—Yarmola, a known poacher, an idle vagabond, whose opinion the village council would never dream of considering—this solicitude of his for the public interest of his native village somehow moved me. I offered to give him lessons myself. What a job it was—my attempt to teach him to read and write! Yarmola, who knew to perfection every path in the forest, almost every tree; who could find his whereabouts day and night, no matter where he was; who could distinguish all the wolves, hares, and foxes of the neighbourhood by their spoor—this same Yarmola could not for the life of him see why, for instance, the letters *m* and *a* together make *ma.* In front of that problem he usually thought painfully for ten minutes and more, and his lean swarthy face with its sunken black eyes, which had been completely absorbed into a stiff black beard and a generous moustache, betrayed an extremity of mental strain.

'Come, Yarmola, say *ma.* Just say *ma* simply,' I urged him. 'Don't look at the paper. Look at me, so. Now say *ma.*'

Yarmola would then heave a deep sigh, put the horn-book on the table, and announce with sad determination:

'No, I can't. . . .'

'Why can't you? It's so easy. Just say *ma* simply, just as I say it.'

'No, sir, I cannot . . . I've forgotten.'

All my methods, my devices and comparisons were being shattered by this monstrous lack of understanding. But Yarmola's longing for knowledge did not weaken at all.

'If I could only write my name!' Yarmola begged me bashfully. 'I don't want anything else. Only my name: Yarmola Popruzhuk—that's all.'

When I finally abandoned the idea of teaching him to read and write properly, I began to show him how to sign his name mechanically. To my amazement this method seemed to be the easiest for Yarmola, and at the end of two months he had very nearly mastered his name. As for his Christian name we had decided to make the task easier by leaving it out altogether.

Every evening, after he had finished filling the stoves, Yarmola waited on patiently until I called him.

'Well, Yarmola, let 's have a go at it,' I would say. He would sidle up to the table, lean on it with his elbows, thrust his pen through his black, shrivelled, stiff fingers, and ask me, raising his eyebrows:

'Shall I write?'

'Yes, write.'

Yarmola drew the first letter quite confidently—P[1]. (This letter was called 'a couple of posts and a crossbeam on top.') Then he looked at me questioningly.

'Why don't you go on writing? Have you forgotten?'

'I 've forgotten.' Yarmola shook his head angrily.

'Heavens, what a fellow you are! Well, make a wheel.'

'Ah, a wheel, a wheel! . . . I know. . . .' Yarmola cheered up, and diligently drew an elongated figure on the paper, in outline very like the Caspian Sea. After this labour he admired the result in silence for some time, bending his head now to the left, then to the right, and screwing up his eyes.

'Why have you stopped there? Go on.'

'Wait a little, sir . . . presently.'

[1] The Russian P is shaped П, as in Greek.

He thought for a couple of minutes and then asked timidly :

'Same as the first ?'

'Right. Just the same.'

So little by little we came to the last letter 'k,' which we knew as 'a stick with a crooked twig tilted sideways in the middle of it.'

'What do you think, sir ?' Yarmola would say sometimes after finishing his work and looking at it with great pride ; 'if I go on learning like this for another five or six months I shall be quite a learned chap. What 's your idea ?'

II

YARMOLA was squatting on his heels in front of the stove door, poking the coals in the stove, while I walked from corner to corner of the room. Of all the twelve rooms of the huge country house I occupied only one—the lounge that used to be. The other rooms were locked up, and there, grave and motionless, mouldered the old brocaded furniture, the rare bronzes, and the eighteenth-century portraits.

The wind was raging round the walls of the house like an old naked, frozen devil. Towards evening the snowstorm became more violent. Some one outside was furiously throwing handfuls of fine dry snow at the window-panes. The forest near by moaned and roared with a dull, hidden, incessant menace. . . .

The wind stole into the empty rooms and the howling chimneys. The old house, weak throughout, full of holes and half decayed, suddenly became alive with strange sounds to which I listened with involuntary anxiety. Into the white drawing-room there broke a deep-drawn sigh, in a sad worn-out voice. In the distance somewhere the dry and rotten floor-boards began to creak under some one's heavy, silent tread. I think that some one in the corridor beside my room is pressing with cautious persistence on the door-handle, and then, suddenly grown furious, rushes all over the house madly shaking all the shutters and doors. Or he gets into the chimney and whines so mournfully, wearily, incessantly—now raising his voice higher and higher, thinner and thinner, all the while, till it becomes a wailing shriek, then lowering it again to a wild beast's growling. Sometimes this terrible guest would rush into my room too, run with a sudden coldness over my back and flicker the lamp flame, which gave a dim light from under a green paper shade, scorched at the top.

There came upon me a strange, vague uneasiness. I thought: Here am I sitting, this bad, stormy night, in a rickety house, in a village lost in woods and snowdrifts, hundreds of miles from town life, from society, from woman's laughter and human conversation. . . . And I began to feel that this stormy evening would drag on for years and tens of years. The wind will whine outside the windows, as it is whining now; the lamp will burn dimly under the paltry green shade, as it burns now; I will walk just as breathlessly up and down my room, and the silent, intent Yarmola will sit so by the stove, a strange creature, alien to me, indifferent to everything in the world, indifferent that his family has nothing to eat, to the raging wind, and my own vague consuming anxiety.

Suddenly I felt an intolerable desire to break this anxious silence with some semblance of a human voice, and I asked:

'Why is there such a wind to-day ? What do you think, Yarmola ?'

'The wind ?' Yarmola muttered, lazily lifting his head. 'Don't you really know ?'

'Of course I don't. How could I ?'

'Truly, you don't know ?' Yarmola livened suddenly. 'I 'll tell you,' he continued with a mysterious note in his voice. 'I 'll tell you this. Either a witch is being born, or a wizard is having a wedding-party.'

'A witch ? . . . Does that mean a sorceress in your place ?'

'Exactly . . . a sorceress.'

I caught up Yarmola eagerly. 'Who knows,' I thought, 'perhaps I 'll manage to get an interesting story out of him presently, all about magic, and buried treasure, and devils.'

'Have you got witches here, in Polyessie ?' I asked.

'I don't know . . . may be,' Yarmola answered with his usual indifference, bending down to the stove again. 'Old folks say there were once. . . . May be it 's not true. . . .'

I was disappointed. Yarmola's characteristic trait was a stubborn silence, and I had already given up hope of getting anything more out of him on this interesting subject. But to my surprise he suddenly began to talk with a lazy indifference as though he was addressing the roaring stove instead of me.

'There was a witch here, five years back. . . . But the boys drove her out of the village.'

'Where did they drive her to ?'

'Where to? Into the forest, of course . . . where else? And they pulled her cottage down as well, so that there shouldn't be a splinter of the cursed den left. . . . And they took her to the cross roads. . . .'

'Why did they treat her like that?'

'She did a great deal of harm. She quarrelled with everybody, poured poison beneath the cottages, tied knots in the corn. . . . Once she asked a village woman for fifteen kopeks. "I haven't got a sixpence," says she. "Right," she says, "I 'll teach you not to give me a sixpence." And what do you think, sir? That very day the woman's child began to be ill. It grew worse and worse and then died. Then it was that the boys drove her out—curse her for a witch.'

'Well . . . where 's the witch now?' I was still curious.

'The witch?' Yarmola slowly repeated the question, as his habit was. 'How should I know?'

'Didn't she leave any relatives in the village?'

'No, not one. She didn't come from our village; she came from the Big Russians, or the gipsies. I was still a tiny boy when she came to our village. She had a little girl with her, a daughter or grandchild. . . . They were both driven out.'

'Doesn't any one go to her now—to get their fortunes told or to get medicine?'

'The womenfolk do,' Yarmola said scornfully.

'Ah. so it 's known where she lives?'

'I don't know. . . . Folks say she lives somewhere near the Devil's Corner. . . . You know the place—the marsh behind the Trine road. She lives in that same marsh. May her mother burn in hell!'

'A witch living ten versts from my house . . . a real live Polyessie witch!' The idea instantly intrigued and excited me.

'Look here, Yarmola,' I said to the forester. 'How could I get to know the witch?'

'Foo!' Yarmola spat in indignation. 'That's a nice thing!'

'Nice or nasty, I'm going to her all the same. As soon as it gets a little warmer, I'll go off at once. You'll come with me, of course?'

Yarmola was so struck by my last words that he jumped right off the floor.

'Me?' he cried indignantly. 'Not for a million! Come what may, I'm not going with you.'

'Nonsense; of course, you'll come.'

'No, sir, I will not . . . not for anything. . . . Me?' he cried again, seized with a new exasperation, 'go to a witch's den? God forbid! And I advise you not to either, sir.'

'As you please. . . . I'll go all the same. . . . I'm very curious to see her.'

'There's nothing curious there,' grunted Yarmola, angrily slamming the door of the stove.

An hour later, when he had taken the samovar off the table and drunk his tea in the dark passage and was preparing to go home, I asked him:

'What 's the witch's name?'

'Manuilikha,' replied Yarmola with sullen rudeness.

Though he had never expressed his feelings, he seemed to have grown greatly attached to me. His affection came from our mutual passion for hunting, from my simple behaviour, the help I occasionally gave his perpetually hungry family, and above all, because I was the only person in the world who did not scold him for his drunkenness—a thing intolerable to Yarmola. That was why my determination to make the acquaintance of the witch put him into such an ugly temper, which he relieved only by sniffing more vigorously, and finally by going off to the back-staircase and kicking his dog Riabchik with all his might. Riabchik jumped aside and began to howl desperately, but immediately ran after Yarmola, still whining.

III

About three days after the weather grew warmer. Very early one morning Yarmola came into my room and said carelessly:

'We shall have to clean the guns, sir.'

'Why?' I asked, stretching myself under the blankets.

'The hares have been busy in the night. There are any amount of tracks. Shall we go after them?'

I saw that Yarmola was waiting impatiently to go to the forest, but he hid his hunter's passion beneath an assumed indifference. In fact, his single-barrelled gun was in the passage already. From that gun not a single woodcock had ever escaped, for all that it was adorned with a few tin patches, and spliced over the places where rust and powder gas had corroded the iron.

No sooner had we entered the forest than we came on a hare's track. The hare broke out into the road, ran about fifty yards along it, and then made a huge leap into the fir plantation.

'Now, we 'll get him in a moment,' Yarmola said. 'Since he 's shown himself, he 'll die here. You go, sir. . . .' He pondered, considering by certain signs known only to himself where he should post me. 'You go to the old inn. And

I 'll get round him from Zanilin. As soon as the dog starts him I 'll give you a shout.'

He disappeared instantly, as it were, plunging into a thick jungle of brushwood. I listened. Not a sound betrayed his poacher movements; not a twig snapped under his feet, in their bast shoes. Without hurrying myself I came to the inn, a ruined and deserted hut, and I stopped on the edge of a young pine forest beneath a tall fir with a straight bare trunk. It was quiet as it can be quiet only in a forest on a windless winter day. The branches were bent with the splendid lumps of snow which clung to them, and made them look wonderful, festive, and cold. Now and then a thin little twig broke off from the top, and with extreme clearness one could hear it as it fell with a tiny cracking noise, touching other twigs in its fall. The snow glinted rose in the sun and blue in the shadow. I fell under the quiet spell of the grave cold silence, and I seemed to feel time passing by me, slowly and noiselessly.

Suddenly far away in the thicket came the sound of Riabchik's bark—the peculiar bark of a dog following a scent, a thin, nervous, trilling bark that passes almost into a squeak. I heard Yarmola's voice immediately, calling angrily after the dog: 'Get him! Get him!' the first word in a long-drawn falsetto, the second in a short bass note.

Judging from the direction of the bark, I thought the dog must be running on my left, and I ran quickly across the meadow to get level with the hare. I hadn't made twenty steps when a huge grey hare jumped out from behind a stump, laid back his long ears and ran leisurely across the road with high delicate leaps, and hid himself in a plantation. After him came Riabchik at full tilt. When he saw me he wagged his tail faintly, snapped at the snow several times with his teeth, and chased the hare again.

Suddenly Yarmola plunged out from the thicket as noiselessly as the dog.

'Why didn't you get across him, sir?' he exclaimed, clicking his tongue reproachfully.

'But it was a long way . . . more than a couple of hundred yards.' Seeing my confusion, Yarmola softened.

'Well, it doesn't matter. . . . He won't get away from us. Go towards the Irenov road. He'll come out there presently.'

I went towards the Irenov road, and in a couple of minutes I heard the dog on a scent again somewhere near me. I was seized with the excitement of the hunt and began to run, keeping my gun down, through a thick shrubbery, breaking the branches and giving no heed to the smart blows they dealt me. I ran for a very long time, and was already beginning to lose my wind, when the dog suddenly stopped barking. I slowed my pace. I had the idea that if I went straight on I should be sure to meet Yarmola on the Irenov road. But I soon realised that I had lost my way as I ran, turning the bushes and the stumps without a thought of where I was going. Then I began to shout to Yarmola. He made no answer.

Meanwhile I was going further. Little by little the forest grew thinner. The ground fell away and became full of little hillocks. The prints of my feet on the snow darkened and filled with water. Several times I sank in it to my knees. I had to jump from hillock to hillock; my feet sank in the thick brown moss which covered them as it were with a soft carpet.

Soon the shrubbery came to an end. In front of me there was a large round swamp, thinly covered with snow; out of the white shroud a few little mounds emerged. Among the trees on the other side of the swamp, the white walls of a hut could be seen. 'It 's the Irenov gamekeeper lives there, probably,' I thought. 'I must go in and ask the way.'

But it was not so easy to reach the hut. Every minute I sank in the bog. My high boots filled with water and made a loud sucking noise at every step, so that I could hardly drag them along.

Finally I managed to get through the marsh, climbed on top of a hillock from whence I could examine the hut thoroughly. It was not even a hut, but one of the chicken-legged erections of the fairy tales. The floor was not built on to the ground, but was raised on piles, probably because of the flood-water which covers all the Irenov forest in the spring. But one of the sides had subsided with age, and this gave the hut a lame and dismal appearance. Some of the window panes were missing; their place was filled by some dirty rags that bellied outwards.

I pressed the latch and opened the door. The room was very dark and violet circles swam before my eyes, which had so long been looking at the snow. For a long time I could not see whether there was any one in the hut.

'Ah! good people, is any one at home?' I asked aloud.

Something moved near the stove. I went closer and saw an old woman, sitting on the floor. A big heap of hen feathers lay before her. The old woman was taking each feather separately, tearing off the down into a basket. The quills she threw on to the floor.

'But it's Manuilikha, the Irenov witch.' The thought flashed into my mind, as soon as I examined her a little more attentively. She had all the features of a witch, according to the folk-tales; her lean hollow cheeks descended to a long, sharp, hanging chin, which almost touched her hook nose. Her sunken, toothless mouth moved incessantly as though she were chewing something. Her faded eyes, once blue, cold, round, protruding, looked exactly like the eyes of a strange, ill-boding bird.

'How d' you do, granny?' I said as affably as I could. 'Your name's Manuilikha, isn't it?'

Something began to bubble and rattle in the old woman's chest by way of reply. Strange sounds came out of her toothless, mumbling mouth, now like the raucous cawing of an ancient crow, then changing abruptly into a hoarse, broken falsetto.

'Once, perhaps, good people called me Manuilikha. . . . But now they call me What 's-her-name, and duck 's the name they gave me. What do *you* want?' she asked in a hostile tone, without interrupting her monotonous occupation.

'You see, I 've lost my way, granny. Do you happen to have any milk?'

'There 's no milk,' the old woman cut me short, angrily. 'There 's a pack of people come straggling about the forest here. . . . You can't keep them all in food and drink. . . .'

'You 're unkind to your guests, granny.'

'Quite true, my dear sir. I 'm quite unkind. We don't keep a store cupboard for you. If you 're tired, sit down a while. Nobody will turn you out. You know what the proverb says: "You can come and sit by our gate, and listen to the noise of a feasting; but we are clever enough to come to you for a dinner." That 's how it is.'

These turns of speech immediately convinced me that the old woman really was a stranger in those parts. The people there have no love for the expressive speech, adorned with curious words, which a Russian of the north so readily displays. Meanwhile the old woman continued her work mechanically, mumbling under her nose, quicker and more indistinctly all the while. I could catch only separate disconnected words. 'There now, Granny Manuilikha. . . . And who he is nobody knows. . . . My years are not a few. . . . He fidgets his feet, chatters and gossips—just like a magpie. . . .'

I listened for some time, and the sudden thought that I was with a mad woman aroused in me a feeling of revolting fear.

However, I had time to catch a glimpse of everything round me. A huge blistered stove occupied the greater part of the hut. There was no icon in the place of honour. On the walls, instead of the customary huntsmen with green moustaches and violet-coloured dogs, and unknown generals, hung bunches of dried herbs, bundles of withered stalks and kitchen utensils. I saw neither owl nor black cat; instead, two speckled fat starlings glanced at me from the stove with a surprised, suspicious air.

'Can't I even have something to drink, granny?' I asked, raising my voice.

'It 's there, in the tub,' the old woman nodded.

The water tasted brackish, of the marsh. Thanking the old woman, though she paid me not the least attention, I asked her how I could get back to the road.

She suddenly lifted up her head, stared at me with her cold birdlike eyes, and murmured hurriedly:

'Go, go . . . young man, go away. You have nothing to do here. There 's a time for guests and a time for none. . . . Go, my dear sir, go.'

So nothing was left to me but to go. But there flashed into my mind a last resource to soften the sternness of the old woman, if only a little. I took out of my pocket a new silver sixpence and held it out to Manuilikha. I was not mistaken ; at the sight of the money the old woman began to stir, her eyes widened, and she stretched out her crooked, knotted, trembling fingers for the coin.

'Oh no, Granny Manuilikha, I shan't give it to you for nothing,' I teased, hiding the coin. 'Tell me my fortune.'

The brown wrinkled face of the witch changed to a discontented grimace. She hesitated and looked irresolutely at my hand that closed over the coin. Her greed prevailed.

'Very well then, come on,' she mumbled, getting up from the floor with difficulty. 'I don't tell anybody's fortune nowadays, my dear. . . . I have forgotten. . . . I am old, my eyes don't see. But I 'll do it for you.'

Holding on to the wall, her bent body shaking at every step, she got to the table, took a pack of dirty cards, thick with age, and pushed them over to me.

'Take the cards, cut with your left hand. . . . Nearest the heart.'

Spitting on her fingers she began to spread the surround. As they fell on the table the cards made a noise like lumps of dough and arranged themselves in a correct eight-pointed star. . . . When the last card fell on its back and covered the king, Manuilikha stretched out her hand to me.

'Cross it with gold, my dear, and you will be happy, you will be rich,' she began to whine in a gipsy beggar's voice.

I pushed the coin I had ready into her hand. Quick as a monkey, the old woman stowed it away in her jaw.

'Something very important is coming to you from afar off,' she began in the usual voluble way. 'A meeting with the queen of diamonds, and some pleasant conversation in an important house. Very soon you will receive unexpected news from the king of clubs. Certain troubles are coming, and then a small legacy. You will be with a number of people; you will get drunk. . . . Not very drunk, but I can see a spree is there. Your life will be a long one. If you don't die when you are sixty-seven, then . . .'

Suddenly she stopped, and lifted up her head as though listening. I listened too. A woman's voice sounded fresh, clear, and strong, approaching the hut singing. And I recognised the words of the charming Little Russian song:

'Ah, is it the blossom or not the bloom
 That bends the little white hazel-tree?
Ah, is it a dream or not a dream
 That bows my little head. . . .'

'Well, now, be off, my dear.' The old woman began to bustle about anxiously, pushing me away from the table. 'You must not be knocking about in other people's huts. Go your way. . . .'

She even seized me by the sleeve of my jacket and pulled me to the door. Her face showed an animal anxiety.

The singing came to an end abruptly, quite

close to the hut. The iron latch rattled loudly, and in the open door a tall laughing girl appeared. With both hands she carefully held up her striped apron, out of which there peeped three tiny birds' heads with red necks and black shiny eyes.

'Look, granny, the finches hopped after me again,' she cried, laughing. 'Look, how funny they are. And, just as if on purpose, I had no bread with me.'

But seeing me she became silent and blushed crimson. Her thick black eyebrows frowned, and her eyes turned questioningly to the old woman.

'The gentleman came in here to ask the way,' the old woman explained. 'Now, dear sir,' she turned to me, with a resolute look, 'you have rested long enough. You have drunk some water, had a chat, and it 's time to go. We are not the folk for you. . . .'

'Look here, my dear,' I said to the girl. 'Please show me the way to the Irenov road; otherwise I 'll stick in this marsh for ever.'

It must have been that the kindly pleading tone in which I spoke impressed her. Carefully she put her little finches on the stove, side by side with the starlings, flung the overcoat which she had already taken off on to the bench, and silently left the hut.

I followed her.

'Are all your birds tame?' I asked, overtaking the girl.

'All tame,' she answered abruptly, not even glancing at me. 'Now look,' she said, stopping by the wattle hedge. 'Do you see the little footpath there, between the fir-trees? Can you see it?'

'Yes, I see.'

'Go straight along it. When you come to the oak stump, turn to your left. You must go straight on through the forest. Then you will come out on the Irenov road.'

All the while she directed me, pointing with her right hand, involuntarily I admired her. There was nothing in her like the local girls, whose faces have such a scared, monotonous look under the ugly head-bands which cover their forehead, mouth, and chin. My unknown was a tall brunette from twenty to twenty-five years old, free and graceful. Her white shirt covered her strong young bosom loosely and charmingly. Once seen, the peculiar beauty of her face could not be forgotten; it was even difficult to get accustomed to it, to describe it. The charm lay in her large, shining, dark eyes, to which the thin arched eyebrows gave an indescribable air, shy, queenly, and innocent, and in the dusky pink of her skin, in the self-willed curl of her lips. Her under-lip was fuller, and it was pushed forward a little, giving her a determined and capricious look.

'Are you really not afraid to live by yourselves in such a lonely spot?' I asked, stopping by the hedge.

She shrugged her shoulders indifferently.

'Why should we be afraid? The wolves do not come near us.'

‘ Wolves are not everything. Your hut might be smothered under the snow. The hut might catch on fire. Anything might happen. You two are there alone, no one could come to your assistance.’

‘ Thank God for that ! ’ she waved her hand scornfully. ‘ If granny and I were left alone entirely, it would be much better, but——’

‘ What ? ’

‘ You will get old, if you want to know so much,’ she cut me short. ‘ And who are you ? ’ she asked anxiously.

I realised that probably the old woman and the girl were afraid of persecution from the authorities, and I hastened to reassure her.

‘ Oh, don’t be alarmed. I ’m not the village policeman, or the clerk, or the exciseman. . . . I ’m not an official at all.’

‘ Is that really true ? ’

‘ On my word of honour. Believe me, I am the most private person. I ’ve simply come to stay here a few months, and then I ’m going away. If you like, I won’t tell a soul that I ’ve been here and seen you. Do you believe me ? ’

The girl’s face brightened a little.

‘ Well, then, if you ’re not lying, you ’re telling the truth. But tell me : had you heard about us, or did you come across us by accident ? ’

‘ I don’t quite know how to explain it myself. . . . Yes, I had heard, and I even wanted to call on you some time. But it was an accident that I came to-day, I lost my way. Now tell me: why are you afraid of people? What harm do they do you?'

She glanced at me with suspicion. But my conscience was clear, and I endured her scrutiny without a tremor. Then she began to speak, with increasing agitation.

'They do bad things. . . . Ordinary people don't matter, but the officials. . . . The village policeman comes—he must be bribed. The inspector—pay again. And before he takes the bribe he insults my grandmother; says she's a witch, a hag, a convict. . . . But what's the good of talking? . . .'

'But don't they touch you?' The imprudent question escaped my lips.

She drew up her head with proud self-confidence, and angry triumph flashed in her half-closed eyes.

'They don't touch me. . . . Once a surveyor came near to me. . . . He wanted a kiss. . . . I don't think he will have forgotten yet how I kissed him.'

So much harsh independence sounded in these proud, derisive words, that I involuntarily thought:

'You haven't been bred in the Polyessie forest for nothing. You're really a dangerous person to joke with. . . .'

'Do we touch anybody?' she continued as her confidence in me grew. 'We do not want people. Once a year I go to the little town to buy soap and salt . . . and some tea for granny.

She loves tea. Otherwise, I could do without them for ever.'

'Well, I see you and your granny are not fond of people. . . . But may I come to see you sometimes for a little while?'

She laughed. How strange and unexpected was the change in her pretty face! There was no trace of her former sternness in it. It had in an instant become bright, shy, and childish.

'Whatever will you do with us? Granny and I are dull. . . . Why, come, if you like, and if you are really a good man. But . . . if you do happen to come, it would be better if you came without a gun. . . .'

'You 're afraid?'

'Why should I be afraid? I 'm afraid of nothing.' Again I could catch in her voice her confidence in her strength. 'But I don't like it. Why do you kill birds, or hares even? They do nobody any harm, and they want to live as much as you or I. I love them; they are so tiny, and such little stupids. . . . Well, good-bye.' She began to hurry. 'I don't know your name. . . . I 'm afraid granny will be cross with me.'

With easy swiftness she ran to the hut. She bent her head, and with her hands caught up her hair, blown loose in the wind.

'Wait, wait a moment,' I called. 'What is your name? Let us be properly introduced.'

'My name 's Alyona. . . . Hereabouts they call me Olyessia.'

I shouldered my gun and went the way I had

been shown. I climbed a small mound from whence a narrow, hardly visible, forest path began, and looked back. Olyessia's red skirt, fluttering in the wind, could still be seen on the steps of the hut, a spot of bright colour on the smooth and blinding background of the snow.

An hour later Yarmola returned. As usual he avoided idle conversation, and asked me not a word of how and where I lost my way. He just said, casually:

'There. . . . I've left a hare in the kitchen. . . . Shall we roast it, or do you want to send it to any one ?'

'But you don't know where I've been today, Yarmola ?' I said, anticipating his surprise.

'How do you mean, I don't know ?' he muttered gruffly. 'You went to the witch's for sure . . .'

'How did you find that out ?'

'How could I help it ? I heard no answer from you, so I went back on your tracks. . . . Sir !' he added in reproachful vexation, 'you shouldn't do such things. . . . It's a sin ! . . .'

IV

THAT year spring came early. It was violent and, as always in Polyessie, unexpected. Brown, shining, turbulent streams began to run down the village streets, foaming angrily round the stones, whirling splinters and feathers along with it. In the huge pools of water was reflected the azure sky, with the round, spinning white clouds that swam in it. Heavy drops pattered noisily from the eaves. Flights of sparrows covered the roadside willows, and chattered with such noisy excitement that nothing could be heard above the clamour. Everywhere was felt the joyous, quick alarm of life.

The snow disappeared. Dirty yellow patches remained here and there in the hollows and the shady thickets. From beneath it peeped the warm wet soil, full of new sap after its winter sleep, full of thirst for a new maternity. Over the black fields swung a light vapour, filling the air with the scent of the thawed earth, with the fresh, penetrating, mighty smell of the spring, which one can distinguish even in the town from a hundred other smells. Together with this scent I felt that the sweet and tender sadness of spring poured into my soul, exuberant with restless expectations and vague presentiments, that romantic sadness which makes all women beautiful in one's eyes, and is always tinged with indefinite regrets for the springs of the past. The nights grew warmer. In their thick moist darkness pulsed the unseen and urgent creation of Nature.

In those spring days the image of Olyessia never left me. Alone, I loved to lie down and close my eyes that I might better concentrate upon her. Continually in my imagination I summoned her up, now stern, now cunning, now with a tender smile resplendent in her face, her young body nurtured on the richness of the old forest to be as harmonious and mighty as a young fir-tree, her fresh voice with its sudden low velvety notes. . . . 'In all her movements, and her words,' I thought, 'there is a nobility, some native grace of modulation.' I was drawn to Olyessia also by the halo of mystery which surrounded her, her superstitious reputation as a witch, her life in the forest thicket amid the marsh, and above all her proud confidence in her own powers, that had shown through the few words she said to me.

Surely there is nothing strange in it that, so soon as the forest paths were dry, I set out for the hut with the chicken legs. In case it should be necessary to placate the querulous old woman I bore with me a half-pound of tea and a few handfuls of sugar.

I found them both at home. The old woman was moving about by the bright burning stove, and Olyessia was sitting on a very tall bench spinning flax. I banged the door as I entered, and she turned round. The thread snapped and the spindle rolled on to the floor.

For some time the old woman stared at me with angry intentness, frowning, and screening her face from the heat of the stove with her hand.

'How do you do, granny?' I said in a loud, hearty voice. 'It must be you don't recognise me. You remember I came in here last month to ask my way? You told me my fortune too.'

'I don't remember anything, sir,' the old woman began to mumble, shaking her head with annoyance. 'I remember nothing. I can't make out at all what you 've forgotten here. We are no company for you. We 're simple, plain folk. . . . There 's nothing for you here. The forest is wide, there 's room enough to wander. . . .'

Taken aback by the hostile reception, and utterly nonplussed, I found myself in the foolish situation of not knowing what to do: whether to turn the rudeness to a joke, or to take offence, or finally to turn and go back without a word. Involuntarily I turned to Olyessia with a look of helplessness. She gave me the faintest trace of a smile of derision, that was not wholly malicious, rose from the spinning-wheel and went to the old woman.

'Don't be afraid, granny,' she said reassuringly. 'He 's not a bad man. He won't do us any harm. Please sit down,' she added, pointing me to a bench in the corner of honour, and paying no more attention to the old woman's grumbling.

Encouraged by her attention, I suddenly decided to adopt the most decisive measures.

'But you do get angry, granny. . . . No sooner does a guest appear in your doorway than you begin to abuse him. And I had brought you a present,' I said, taking the parcels out of my bag.

The old woman threw a swift glance at the parcels; but instantly turned her back upon me.

Immediately, I handed her the tea and sugar. This soothed the old woman somewhat, for though she continued to grumble, it was no longer in the old implacable tone. Olyessia sat down to her yarn again, and I placed myself near to her, on a small, low, rickety stool. With her left hand Olyessia was swiftly twisting a white thread of flax, silky soft, and in her right the spindle whirled with an easy humming. Now she would let it fall almost to the floor; then she would catch it neatly, and with a quick movement of her fingers send it spinning round again. In her hands this work (which at the first glance appears so simple, but in truth demands the habit and dexterity of centuries), went like lightning. I could not help turning my eyes to those hands. They were coarsened and blackened by the work, but they were small and of shape so beautiful that many a princess would have envied them.

'You never told me that granny had told your fortune,' said Olyessia, and, seeing that I gave a cautious glance behind me, she added: 'It's quite all right, she 's rather deaf. She won't hear. It 's only my voice she understands well.'

'Yes, she did. Why ?'

'I just asked . . . nothing more. . . . And do you believe in it ?' She gave a quick, stealthy glance.

'Believe what ? The fortune your granny told me, or generally ?'

'I mean generally.'

'I don't quite know. It would be truer to say, I don't believe in it, but still who knows ? They say there are cases. . . . They write about it in clever books even. But I don't believe what your granny told me at all. Any village woman could tell me as much.'

Olyessia smiled.

'Yes, nowadays she tells fortunes badly, it 's true. She 's old, and besides she 's very much afraid. But what did the cards say ?'

'Nothing interesting. I can't even remember it now. The usual kind of thing : a distant journey, something with clubs. . . . I 've quite forgotten.'

'Yes, she 's a bad fortune-teller now. She 's grown so old that she has forgotten a great many words. . . . How could she ? And she 's scared as well. It 's only the sight of money makes her consent to tell.'

'What 's she scared of ?'

'The authorities, of course. . . . The village policeman comes, and threatens her every time. "I can have you put away at any minute," he says. "You know what people like you get for witchcraft? Penal servitude for life on Hawk Island." Tell me what you think. Is it true?'

'It's not altogether a lie. There is some punishment for doing it, but not so bad as all that. . . . And you, Olyessia, can you tell fortunes?'

It was as though she were perplexed, but only for a second.

'I can. . . . But not for money,' she added hastily.

'You might put out the cards for me?'

'No,' she answered with quiet resolution, shaking her head.

'Why won't you? Very well, some other time. . . . Somehow I believe you will tell me the truth.'

'No. I will not. I won't do it for anything.'

'Oh, that's not right, Olyessia. For first acquaintance' sake you can't refuse. . . . Why don't you want to?'

'Because I've put out the cards for you already. It's wrong to do it twice.'

'Wrong? But why? I don't understand it.'

'No, no, it's wrong, wrong,' she began to whisper with superstitious dread. 'It's forbidden to ask twice of Fate. It's not right. Fate will discover, overhear. . . . She does not like to be asked. That's why all fortune-tellers are unhappy.'

I wanted to make a jesting reply to Olyessia; but I could not. There was too much sincere conviction in her words; and when she turned her head to the door in a strange fear as she uttered the word Fate, in spite of myself I turned with her.

'Well, if you won't want to tell me my fortune now, tell me what the cards have told you already,' I begged.

Olyessia suddenly gave a turn to the spinning-wheel, and with her hand touched mine.

'No! . . . better not,' she said. A childlike, imploring look came into her eyes. 'Please, don't ask me. . . . There was nothing good in it. . . . Better not ask.'

But I insisted. I could not understand whether her refusal and her dark allusions to Fate were the deliberate trick of a fortune-teller, or whether she herself really believed what she said. But I became rather uneasy; what was almost a dread took hold of me.

'Well, I 'll tell you, perhaps,' Olyessia finally consented. 'But listen; a bargain 's better than money; don't be angry if you don't like what I say. The cards said that though you are a good man, you are only a weak one. . . . Your goodness is not sound, nor quite sincere. You are not master of your word. You love to have the whip-hand of people, and yet, though you yourself do not want to, you submit to them. You are fond of wine and—— Well, if I 've got to say, I 'll say everything right to the last. . . . You are very fond of women, and because of that you will have much evil in your life. . . . You do not value money and you cannot save. You will never be rich. . . . Shall I go on?'

'Go on, go on, say everything you know!'

'The cards said too that your life will not be a happy one. You will never love with your heart, because your heart is cold and dull, and you will cause great sorrow to those who love you. You will never marry; you will die a bachelor. There will be no great joys in your life, but much weariness and depression. . . . There will come a time when you will want to put an end to your life. . . . That will come to you, but you will not dare, you will go on enduring. You will suffer great poverty, but towards the end your fate will be changed through the death of some one near you, quite unexpected. But all this will be in years to come; but this year . . . I don't know exactly when . . . the cards say very soon . . . maybe this very month——'

'What will happen this year?' I asked when she stopped again.

'I'm afraid to tell you any more. . . . A great love will come to you through the queen of clubs. Only I can't see whether she is married or a girl, but I know that she has dark hair. . . .'

Involuntarily I gave a swift glance to Olyessia's head.

'Why are you looking at me?' she blushed suddenly, feeling my glance, with the sensitiveness peculiar to some women. 'Well, yes, something like mine,' she continued, mechanically arranging her hair, and blushing still more.

'So you say, a great love from clubs?' I laughed.

'Don't laugh. It's no use laughing,' Olyessia said seriously, almost sternly. 'I'm only telling you the truth.'

'Well, I won't laugh any more, I promise. What is there more?'

'More. . . . Oh! Evil will come upon the queen of clubs, worse than death. She will suffer a great disgrace through you, one that she will never be able to forget; she will have an everlasting sorrow. . . . In her planet no harm comes to you.'

'Tell me, Olyessia. Couldn't the cards deceive you? Why should I do so many unpleasant things to the queen of clubs? I am a quiet unassuming fellow, yet you've said so many awful things about me.'

'I don't know that. . . . The cards showed that it's not you will do it—I mean, not on purpose—but all this misfortune will come through you. . . . You'll remember my words, when they come true.'

'The cards told you all this, Olyessia?'

She did not answer at once, and then as though evasive and reluctant:

'The cards as well. . . . But even without them I learn a great deal, just by the face alone. If, for instance, some one is going to die soon by an ugly death, I can read it immediately in his face. I need not speak to him, even.'

'What do you see in his face?'

'I don't know myself. I suddenly feel afraid,

as though he were a dead man standing before me. Just ask granny, she will tell you that it 's the truth I 'm saying. The year before last, Trophim the miller hung himself in his mill. Only two days before I saw him and said to granny: "Just look, granny, Trophim will die an ugly death soon." And so it was. Again, last Christmas Yashka the horse thief came to us and asked granny to tell his fortune. Granny put out the cards for him and began. He asked, joking: "Tell me what sort of death will I have?" and he laughed. The moment I glanced at him, I could not move. I saw Yashka sitting there, but his face was dead, green. . . . His eyes were shut, his lips black. . . . A week afterwards we heard that the peasants had caught Yashka just as he was trying to take some horses off. . . . They beat him all night long. . . . They are bad people here, merciless. . . . They drove nails into his heels, smashed his ribs with stakes, and he gave up the ghost about dawn.'

'Why didn't you tell him that misfortune was waiting for him?'

'Why should I tell?' Olyessia replied. 'Can a man escape what Fate has doomed? It is useless for a man to be anxious the last days of his life. . . . And I loathe myself for seeing these things. I am disgusted with my own self. . . . But what can I do? It is mine by Fate. When granny was younger she could see Death, too; so could my mother and granny's mother—we are not responsible. It is in our blood. . . .'

She left off her spinning, bent her head and quietly placed her hands upon her knees. In her arrested, immobile eyes and her wide pupils was reflected some dark terror, an involuntary submission to mysterious powers and supernatural knowledge which cast a shadow upon her soul.

V

THEN the old woman spread a clean cloth with embroidered ends on the table, and placed a steaming pot upon it.

'Come to supper, Olyessia,' she called to her granddaughter, and after a moment's hesitation added, turning to me: 'Perhaps you will eat with us too, sir? Our food is very plain; we have no soup, only plain groats. . . .'

I cannot say there was any particular insistence in her invitation, and I was already minded to refuse had not Olyessia in her turn invited me with such simplicity and a smile so kind, that in spite of myself I agreed. She herself poured me out a plateful of groats, a porridge of buckwheat and fat, onion, potato and chicken, an amazingly tasty and nourishing dish. Neither grandmother nor granddaughter crossed themselves as they sat down to table. During supper I continually watched both women, because up till now I have retained a deep conviction that a person is nowhere revealed so clearly as when he eats. The old woman swallowed the porridge with hasty greed, chewing aloud and pushing large pieces of bread into her mouth, so that big lumps rose and moved beneath her flabby cheeks. In Olyessia's manner of eating even there was a native grace.

An hour later, after supper, I took my leave of my hostesses of the chicken-legged hut.

'I will walk with you a little way, if you like,' Olyessia offered.

'What 's this walking out you 're after ?' the old woman mumbled angrily. 'You can't stay in your place, you gad-fly. . . .'

But Olyessia had already put a red cashmere shawl on. Suddenly she ran up to her grandmother, embraced her and gave her a loud kiss.

'Dear little precious granny. . . . It 's only a moment. I 'll be back in a second.'

'Very well, then, madcap.' The old woman feebly wrenched herself away. 'Don't misunderstand her, sir ; she 's very stupid.'

Passing a narrow path we came out into the forest road, black with mud, all churned with hoof marks and rutted with wheel tracks, full of water, in which the fire of the evening star was reflected. We walked at the side of the road, covered everywhere with the brown leaves of last year, not yet dry after the snow. Here and there through the dead yellow big wakening blue-bells—the earliest flowers in Polyessie—lifted their lilac heads.

'Listen, Olyessia,' I began ; 'I very much want to ask you something, but I am afraid you will be cross. . . . Tell me, is it true what they say about your grandmother ? . . . How shall I express it ?'

'She 's a witch ?' Olyessia quietly helped me out.

'No. . . . Not a witch,' I caught her up.

'Well, yes, a witch if you like. . . . Certainly, people say such things. Why shouldn't one know certain herbs, remedies, and charms ? . . . But if you find it unpleasant, you need not answer.'

'But why not ?' she answered simply. 'Where's the unpleasantness ? Yes, it's true, she's a witch. But now she's grown old and can no longer do what she did before.'

'And what did she do before ?' I was curious.

'All kinds of things. She could cure illness, heal toothache, put a spell on a mine, pray over any one who was bitten by a mad dog or a snake, she could find out treasure trove. . . . It is impossible to tell one everything.'

'You know, Olyessia, you must forgive me, but I don't believe it all. Be frank with me. I shan't tell anybody ; but surely this is all a pretence in order to mystify people ?'

She shrugged her shoulders indifferently.

'Think what you like. Of course, it's easy to mystify a woman from the village, but I wouldn't deceive you.'

'You really believe in witchcraft, then ?'

'How could I disbelieve ? Charms are in our destiny. I can do a great deal myself.'

'Olyessia, darling, . . . if you only knew how interested I was. . . . Won't you really show me anything ?'

'I'll show you, if you like.' Olyessia readily consented. 'Would you like me to do it now ?'

'Yes, at once, if possible.'

'You won't be afraid ?'

'What next? I might be afraid at night perhaps, but it is still daylight.'

'Very well. Give me your hand.'

I obeyed. Olyessia quickly turned up the sleeve of my overcoat and unfastened the button of my cuff. Then she took a small Finnish knife about three inches long out of her pocket, and removed it from its leather case.

'What are you going to do?' I asked, for a mean fear had awakened in me.

'You will see immediately. . . . But you said you wouldn't be afraid.'

Suddenly her hand made a slight movement, hardly perceptible. I felt the prick of the sharp blade in the soft part of my arm a little higher than the pulse. Instantly blood showed along the whole width of the cut, flowed over my hand, and began to drop quickly on to the earth. I could hardly restrain a cry, and I believe I grew pale.

'Don't be afraid. You won't die,' Olyessia smiled.

She seized my arm above the cut, bent her face down upon it, and began to whisper something quickly, covering my skin with her steady breathing. When she stood up again unclasping her fingers, on the wounded place only a red graze remained.

'Well, have you had enough?' she asked with a sly smile, putting her little knife away. 'Would you like some more?'

'Certainly, I would. Only if possible not quite so terrible and without bloodshed, please.'

'What shall I show you?' she mused. 'Well, this will do. Walk along the road in front of me. But don't look back.'

'This won't be terrible?' I asked, trying to conceal my timid apprehensions of an unpleasant surprise with a careless smile.

'No, no. . . . Quite trifling. . . . Go on.'

I went ahead, very much intrigued by the experiment, feeling Olyessia's steady glance behind my back. But after about a dozen steps I suddenly stumbled on a perfectly even piece of ground and fell flat.

'Go on, go on!' cried Olyessia. 'Don't look back! It's nothing at all. It will be all right before your wedding day. . . . Keep a better grip on the ground next time, when you're going to fall.'

I went on. Another ten steps, and a second time I fell my full length.

Olyessia began to laugh aloud and to clap her hands.

'Well, are you satisfied now?' she cried, her white teeth gleaming. 'Do you believe it now? It's nothing, nothing. . . . You flew down instead of up.'

'How did you manage that?' I asked in surprise, shaking the little clinging twigs and blades of grass from my clothes. 'Is it a secret?'

'Not at all. I'll tell you with pleasure. Only I'm afraid that perhaps you won't understand. . . . I shan't be able to explain. . . .'

Indeed, I did not understand her altogether.

But, as far as I can make out, this odd trick consists in her following my footsteps, step by step, in time with me. She looks at me steadily, trying to imitate my every movement down to the least; as it were, she identifies herself with me. After a few steps she begins to imagine a rope drawn across the road a certain distance in front of me—a yard from the ground. The moment my foot is touching this imaginary rope, Olyessia suddenly pretends to fall, and then, as she says, the strongest man must infallibly fall. . . . I remembered Olyessia's confused explanation long afterwards when I read Charcot's report on the experiments which he made on two women patients in the Salpêtrière, who were professional witches suffering from hysteria. I was greatly surprised to discover that French witches who came from the common people employed exactly the same science in the same cases as the beautiful witch of Polyessie.

'Oh, I can do a great many things besides,' Olyessia boldly declared. 'For instance, I can put a fear into you. . . .'

'What does that mean?'

'I 'll act so that you feel a great dread. Suppose you are sitting in your room in the evening. Suddenly for no reason at all such a fear will take hold of you that you will begin to tremble and won't dare to turn round. But for this I must know where you live and see your room beforehand.'

'Well, that 's quite a simple affair.' I was sceptical. 'You only have to come close to the window, tap on it, call out something or other. . . .'

'Oh no! . . . I shall be in the forest at the time. I won't go out of the hut. . . . But I will sit down and think all the while: I'll think that I am walking along the road, entering your house, opening the door, coming into your room. . . . You're sitting somewhere; at the table, say. . . . I walk up to you from behind quietly and stealthily. . . . You don't hear me. . . . I seize your shoulder with my hands and begin to squeeze . . . stronger, stronger, stronger. . . . I stare at you, just like this. Look! . . .'

Her thin eyebrows suddenly closed together. Her eyes were fixed upon me in a stare, fascinating, threatening. Her pupils dilated and became blue. Instantly I remembered a Medusa's head, the work of a painter I have forgotten, in the Trietyakov Gallery in Moscow. Beneath this strange look I was seized by a cold terror of the supernatural.

'Well, that'll do, Olyessia. . . . That's enough,' I said with a forced laugh. 'I much prefer you when you smile. Your face is so kind and childlike.'

We went on. I suddenly recollected the expressiveness of Olyessia's conversation—elegance even for a simple girl—and I said:

'Do you know what surprises me in you, Olyessia? You've grown up in the forest without seeing a soul. . . . Of course, you can't read very much. . . .'

'I can't read at all.'

'Well, that makes it all the more. . . . Yet you speak as well as a real lady. Tell me, where did you learn it? You understand what I mean?'

'Yes, I understand. It 's from granny. You mustn't judge her by her appearance. She is so clever! Some day she may speak when you are there, when she has become used to you. She knows everything, everything on earth that you can ask her. It 's true she 's old now.'

'Then she has seen a great deal in her lifetime. Where does she come from? Where did she live before?'

It seemed that these questions did not please Olyessia. She hesitated to answer, evasive and reluctant.

'I don't know. . . . She doesn't like to talk of that herself. If ever she says anything about it, she asks you to forget it, to put it quite out of mind. . . . But it 's time for me. . . .' Olyessia hastened, 'Granny will be cross. Good-bye. . . . Forgive me, but I don't know your name.'

I gave her my name.

'Ivan Timofeyevich? Well, that 's all right. Good-bye, Ivan Timofeyevich! Don't disdain our hut. Come sometimes.'

I held out my hand at parting, and her small strong hand responded with a vigorous friendly grip.

VI

FROM that day I began to be a frequent visitor to the chicken-legged house. Every time I came Olyessia met me with her usual dignified reserve. But I always could tell, by the first involuntary she made on seeing me, that she was glad that I had come. The old woman still went on grumbling as she used, muttering under her nose, but she expressed no open malevolence, owing to her granddaughter's intercession, of which I was certain though I had not witnessed it. Also, the presents I would bring her from time to time made a considerable impression in my favour—a warm shawl, a pot of jam, a bottle of cherry brandy. As though by tacit consent, Olyessia began to make a habit of accompanying me as far as the Irenov road as I went home. And there always began such a lively interesting conversation, that involuntarily we both made an effort to prolong the journey, walking as slowly as possible in the silent fringes of the forest. When we came to the Irenov road, I went back half a mile with her, and even then before we parted we would stand talking for a long while beneath the fragrant shade of the pine branches.

It was not only Olyessia's beauty that fascinated me, but her whole free independent nature, her mind at once clear and enwrapped in unshakable ancestral superstitions, childlike and innocent, yet not wholly devoid of the sly coquetry of the handsome woman. She never tired of asking me every detail concerning things which stirred her bright unspoiled imagination—countries and peoples, natural phenomena, the order of the earth and the universe, learned men, large towns. . . . Many things seemed to her wonderful, fairy, incredible. But from the very beginning of our acquaintance I took such a serious, sincere, and simple tone with her that she readily put a complete trust in all my stories. Sometimes when I was at a loss for an explanation of something which I thought was too difficult for her half-savage mind—it was often by no means clear to my own,—I answered her eager questions with, 'You see. . . . I shan't be able to explain this to you. . . . You won't understand me.'

Then she would begin to entreat me.

'Please tell me, please, I 'll try. . . . Tell me somehow, though . . . even if it 's not clear.'

She forced me to have recourse to preposterous comparisons and incredibly bold analogies, and when I was at a loss for a suitable expression she would help me out with a torrent of impatient conclusions, like those which we offer to a stammerer. And indeed in the end her pliant mobile mind and her fresh imagination triumphed over my pedagogic impotence. I became convinced that, considering her environment and her education (rather, lack of education) her abilities were amazing.

Once I happened in passing to mention Petersburg. Olyessia was instantly intrigued.

'What is Petersburg? A small town?'

'No, it's not a small one. It's the biggest Russian city.'

'The biggest? The very largest of all? There isn't one bigger?' she insisted naïvely.

'The largest of all. The chief authorities live there . . . the big folks. The houses there are all made of stone; there aren't any wooden ones.'

'Of course, it's much bigger than our Stiepany?' Olyessia asked confidently.

'Oh, yes. A good bit bigger. Say five hundred times as big. There are houses there so big that twice as many people live in a single one of them as in the whole of Stiepany.'

'My God! What kind of houses can they be?' Olyessia asked almost in fright.

'Terrible houses. Five, six, even seven stories. You see that fir tree there?'

'The tall one. I see.'

'Houses as tall as that, and they're crammed with people from top to bottom. The people live in wretched little holes, like birds in cages, ten people in each, so that there isn't enough air to breathe. Some of them live downstairs, right under the earth, in the damp and cold. They don't see the sun from one end of the year to the other, some of them.'

'Nothing would make me change my forest for your city,' Olyessia said, shaking her head. 'Even when I go to the market at Stiepany, I'm disgusted. They push, shout, swear . . .

and I have such a longing for the forest, that I want to throw everything away and run and never look back. God may have your city: I don't want to live there.'

'But what if your husband comes from a town?' I asked with the trace of a smile.

Her eyebrows frowned and her nostrils trembled.

'What next!' she said with scorn. 'I don't want a husband.'

'You say that now, Olyessia. Nearly every girl says the same, but still they marry. You wait a bit: you'll meet somebody and you'll fall in love—and you'll follow him, not only to town, but to the end of the earth.'

'No, no. . . . We won't talk of that, please,' she cut me short in vexation. 'Why should we talk like this? I ask you not to.'

'How funny you are, Olyessia. Do you really believe you'll never love a man in your life? You're so young, handsome, strong. If your blood once catches fire, no oaths of yours will help you.'

'Well, . . . then, I'll love,' Olyessia answered with a challenge in her flashing eyes. 'I shan't ask anybody's leave.'

'So you'll have to marry too,' I teased her.

'I suppose you're meaning the church?' she guessed.

'Exactly—the church. The priest will lead you round the altar; the deacon will sing, "Isaiah, rejoice!" they'll put a crown on your head. . . .'

Olyessia cast down her eyes and shook her head, faintly smiling.

'No, dear. . . . Perhaps you won't like what I say, but in our family no one was ever married in church. My mother and my grandmother before her managed to live without that. . . . Besides, we must not enter a church. . . .'

'All because of your witchery ?'

'Yes, because of our witchery,' Olyessia replied with a calm seriousness. 'How could I dare to appear in a church ? From my very birth my soul was sold to *Him*.'

'Olyessia, dear. . . . Believe me, you 're deceiving yourself. It 's wild and ridiculous what you say.'

Once more there appeared on Olyessia's face the strange expression of convinced and gloomy submissiveness to her mysterious destiny, which I had noticed before.

'No, no. . . . You can't understand it. . . . But I feel it. . . . Just here. . . .' She pressed her hand strongly to her heart. 'I feel it in my soul. All our family is cursed for ever and ever. But think yourself, who is it that helps us if it is not *He* ? Can an ordinary person do the things I can do ? All our power comes from *Him*.'

Every time our conversation touched upon this strange theme it ended in the same way. In vain I exhausted every argument to which Olyessia was sensible ; in vain I spoke in simple terms of hypnotism, suggestion, mental doctors, and Indian fakirs : in vain I endeavoured to explain certain of her experiments by physiology, such, for instance, as blood charming, which is easily produced by skilful pressure on a vein. Still Olyessia, who believed me so implicitly in all else, refuted all my arguments and explanations with obstinate insistence.

'Very well, I 'll make you a present of blood charming,' she said, raising her voice in the heat of the discussion. 'But where do the other things come from? Is blood charming the only thing I know? Would you like me to take away all the mice and beetles from a hut in a single day? If you like, I 'll cure the most violent fever in two days with plain cold water, even though all your doctors give the patient up. I can make you forget any word you like, completely? And how is it I interpret dreams? How is it I can see the future?'

The discussion always ended by our mutual silence, from which a certain inward irritation against each other was not wholly absent. Indeed, for much of her black art I could find no explanation in my small science. I do not know and cannot say whether Olyessia possessed one half the secrets of which she spoke with such naïve belief. But the things which I frequently witnessed planted an unshakable conviction in me that Olyessia had access to that strange knowledge, unconscious, instinctive, dim, acquired only by accidental experience, which has outrun exact science for centuries, and lives intertwined with wild and ridiculous superstitions, in the obscure impenetrable heart of the masses, where it is transmitted from one generation to another as the greatest of all secrets.

For all our disagreement on this single point, we became more and more strongly attached to one another. Not a word had been spoken between us of love as yet, but it had become a necessity for us to be together; and often in moments of silence I saw Olyessia's eyes moisten, and a thin blue vein on her temple begin to pulse.

But my relations with Yarmola were quite ruined. Evidently my visits to the chicken-legged hut were no secret to him, nor were my evening walks with Olyessia. With amazing exactness, he always knew everything that went on in the forest. For some time I noticed that he had begun to avoid me. His black eyes watched me from a distance, with reproach and discontent every time I went out to walk in the forest, though he did not express his reproof by so much as a single word. Our comically serious studies in reading and writing came to an end; and if I occasionally called Yarmola in to learn during the evening he would only wave his hand.

'What 's the good? It 's a peggling business, sir!' he would say with lazy contempt.

Our hunting also ceased. Every time I began to talk of it, Yarmola found some excuse or other for refusing. Either his gun was out of order, or his dog was ill, or he was too busy. 'I have no time, sir. . . . I have to be ploughing to-day,' was Yarmola's usual answer to my invitation; but I knew quite well that he would do no ploughing at all, but spend a good hour outside the inn in the doubtful hope of somebody standing him a drink. This silent, concealed animosity began to weary me, and I began to think of dispensing with Yarmola's services, on the first suitable occasion. . . . I was restrained only by a sense of pity for his enormous poverty-stricken family, whom Yarmola's four weekly roubles just saved from starvation.

VII

ONCE when I came to the chicken-legged hut, as my habit was, just before dark, I was immediately struck by the anxiety of its occupants. The old woman sat with her feet on the bed, hunched up, and swayed to and fro with her head in her hands, murmuring something I could not catch. She paid no attention to my greeting. Olyessia welcomed me kindly as always, but our conversation made no headway. She listened to me absently and answered me inconsequently. On her beautiful face lay the shadow of some unceasing secret trouble.

'Something bad has happened to you, Olyessia, I can see,' I said cautiously, touching her hand which lay on the bench.

Olyessia quickly turned her face to the window, as though she were examining something. She tried to look calm, but her eyebrows drew together and trembled, and her teeth violently bit her under lip.

'No, . . . what could have happened to us?' she said with a dull voice. 'Everything is just as it was.'

'Olyessia, why don't you tell me the truth? It's wrong of you. . . . I thought that we had become real friends.'

'It's nothing, really. . . . Nothing. . . . Our troubles . . . trifles.'

'No, Olyessia, they don't seem to be trifles. You 're not like yourself.'

'That 's only your fancy.'

'Be frank with me, Olyessia. I don't know whether I can help, but I can give you some advice perhaps. . . . And, anyhow, you 'll feel better when you 've shared your trouble.'

'But it 's really not worth talking about,' Olyessia replied impatiently. 'You can't possibly help us at all, now.'

Suddenly, with unexpected passion, the old woman broke into the conversation.

'Why are you so stubborn, you little fool? Some one talks business to you, and you hold up your nose. As if nobody in the world was cleverer than you! If you please, sir, I 'll tell you the whole story,' she said, turning towards me, 'beginning with the beginning.'

The trouble appeared much more considerable than I could have supposed from Olyessia's proud words. The evening before, the local policeman had come to the chicken-legged hut.

'First he sat down, nice and politely, and asked for vodka,' Manuilikha said, 'and then he began and went on and on. "Clear out of the hut in twenty-four hours with all your belongings. If I come next time," he says, "and find you here, then I tell you, you 'll go to jail. I 'll send you away with a couple of soldiers to your native place, curse you." But you know, sir, my native place is hundreds of miles away, the town of Amchensk. . . . I haven't a soul there now who knows me. Our passports have been out of date for years, and besides they aren't in order. Ah, my God, what misfortune!'

'Then why did he let you live here before, and only just now made up his mind?'

'How can I tell? . . . He shouted out something or other, but I confess I couldn't understand it. You see how it is: this hole we live in isn't ours. It belongs to the landlord. Olyessia and I used to live in the village before, but the——'

'Yes, yes, I know, granny. I've heard about that. The peasants got angry with you——'

'That's it, exactly. So I begged this hut from the old landlord, Mr. Abrossimov. Now, they say a new landlord has bought the forest, and it seems he wants to drain some marshes. But what can I do?'

'Perhaps it's all a lie, granny,' I said. 'And the sergeant only wants to get a pound out of you.'

'But I offered it to him, I offered it, sir. He wouldn't take it. It's a strange business. . . . I offered him three pounds, but he wouldn't take it. . . . It was awful. He swore at me so badly that I didn't know where I was. All the while he went on saying: "Be off with you, be off!" What can we do now? We're alone in the world. Good sir, you might manage to help us in some way. You could speak to him; his belly's never satisfied. I 'm sure I 'd be grateful to you eternally.'

'Granny!' said Olyessia, in a slow reproachful voice.

'What do you mean, "Granny!"' The old woman was annoyed. 'Twenty-five years I 've been a granny to you. And what 's your opinion; it 's better to carry a beggar's pack? No, don't listen to her, sir! Of your charity, do something for us if you can.'

I gave her vague promises to take some steps, though, to tell the truth I could see but little hope. If our sergeant wouldn't take money, then the affair must be very serious. That evening Olyessia parted from me coldly, and, quite against her usual habit, did not walk with me. I could see that the proud girl was angry with me for interfering, and rather ashamed of her grandmother's whimpering.

VIII

It was a warm, greyish morning. Several times already there had been brief showers of heavy fruitful rain, which makes the young grass grow before your eyes and the new shoots stretch out. After the rain the sun peeped out for a moment, pouring its joyous glitter over the tender green of the lilac bushes, sodden with the rain, which made all my hedge. The sparrows' impetuous chirrup grew louder among the lush garden-beds, and the scent of the sticky brown poplar buds came sweeter. I was sitting at the table, drawing a plan of timber to be felled, when Yarmola entered the room.

'The sergeant 's here,' he said gloomily.

At the moment I had completely forgotten that I had ordered him a couple of days ago to let me know in case the sergeant were to pass. It was impossible for me to understand immediately what was the connection between me and the delegate of authority.

'What?' I said in confusion.

'I say the sergeant 's here,' Yarmola repeated in the same hostile tone that he normally assumed towards me during the last days. 'I saw him on the dam just now. He's coming here.'

There was a rumble of wheels on the road outside. A long thin chocolate-coloured gelding with a hanging under lip, and an insulted look on its face, gravely trotted up with a tall, jolting, basket gig. There was only a single trace. The place of the other was supplied by a piece of stout rope. (Malicious tongues asserted that the sergeant had put this miserable contraption together on purpose to avoid any undesirable comments.) The sergeant himself held the reins, filling both seats with his enormous body, which was wrapped in a grey uniform made of smart military cloth.

'Good-day to you, Evpsychyi Afrikanovich!' I called, leaning out of the window.

'Ah, good-day! How do you do?' he answered in a loud, courteous, official baritone.

He drew up his horse, saluted with straightened palm, and bent his body forward with elephantine grace.

'Come in for a moment. I've got a little business with you.'

The sergeant spread his hands wide and shook his head.

'Can't possibly. I'm on duty. I've got to go to Volocha for an inquest—man drowned.'

But I knew Evpsychyi's weak points; so I said with assumed indifference:

'It's a pity . . . a great pity . . . and I've got a couple of bottles of the best from Count Vortzel's cellar. . . .'

'Can't manage it. . . . Duty.'

'The butler sold them to me, because he's an acquaintance of mine. He'd brought them up in the cellar, like his own children. . . . You ought to come in. . . . I 'll tell them to give the horse a feed.'

'You 're a nice one, you are,' the sergeant said in reproof. 'Don't you know that duty comes first of all ? . . . What 's in the bottles, though ? Plum wine ?'

'Plum wine ! ' I waved my hand. 'It 's the real old stuff, that 's what it is, my dear sir ! '

'I must confess I 've just had a bite and a drop.' The sergeant scratched his cheek regretfully, wrinkling his face incredibly.

I continued with the same calm.

'I don't know whether it 's true ; but the butler swore it was two hundred years old. It smells just like an old cognac, and it 's as yellow as amber.'

'Ah, what are you doing with me ?' said the sergeant. 'Who 'll hold my horse ?'

I really had some bottles of the old liqueur, though it was not quite so old as I made out ; but I thought that suggestion might easily add a hundred years to its age. . . . At any rate it was the real home-distilled, omnipotent stuff, the pride of a ruined magnate's cellar. (Evpsychyi Afrikanovich, who was the son of a parson, immediately begged a bottle from me, in case, as he put it, he were to catch a bad cold.) Besides, I had some very conducive *hors d'œuvre*: young radishes, with fresh churned butter.

'Now, what 's the little business ?' the sergeant asked after his fifth glass, throwing himself back in the old chair which groaned under him.

I began to explain the position of the poor old woman ; I dwelt on her hopeless despair ; spoke lightly of useless formalities. The sergeant listened to me with his head bent down, methodically clearing the small roots from the succulent red radishes, and chewing and crunching them with relish. Now and then he gave me a quick glance with his cloudy, indifferent, preposterously little blue eyes; but I could read nothing on his great red face, neither sympathy nor opposition. When I finally became silent, he only asked.

'Well, what is it you want from me ?'

'What do you mean ?' I became agitated. 'Look at their position, please—two poor defenceless women living there——'

'And one of them 's a perfect little bud ! ' the sergeant put in maliciously.

'Bud or no bud—that doesn't come into it. But why shouldn't you take some interest in them ? As though you really need to turn them out in such a hurry ? Just wait a day or two until I 've been to the landlord. What do you stand to lose, even if you waited for a month ?'

'What do I stand to lose ?' The sergeant rose in his chair. 'Good God ! I stand to lose everything—my job, first of all. Who knows what sort of a man this new landlord, Ilyashevich is ? Perhaps he 's an underhand devil, one of the sort who get hold of a bit of paper and a pen on the slightest provocation, and send a little report to Petersburg ? There are men of the kind !'

I tried to reassure the agitated sergeant.

'That 's enough, Evpsychyi Afrikanovich! You 're exaggerating the whole affair. After all, a risk 's a risk, and gratitude 's gratitude.'

'Ph-e-w!' The sergeant gave a long-drawn whistle and thrust his hands into his trouser-pockets. 'It 's gratitude, is it? Do you think I 'm going to stake my official position for three pounds? No, you 've got a wrong idea of me.'

'But what are you getting warm about, Evpsychyi Afrikanovich? The amount isn't the point, just simply—well, let 's say, for humanity's sake——'

'For hu-man-i-ty's sake?' He hammered out each syllable. 'I 'm full up to here with your humanity!' He tapped vigorously on the bronzed nape of his mighty neck which hung down over his collar in a fat, hairless fold.

'That 's a bit too strong, Evpsychyi Afrikanovich.'

'Not a bit too strong! "They 're the plague of the place," as Mr. Krylov, the famous fable-writer, said. That 's what these two ladies are. You don't happen to have read that splendid work, by His Excellency Count Urussov, called *The Police Sergeant*?'

'No, I haven't.'

'Well, you ought to have. A brilliant work, highly moral. I would advise you to make its acquaintance when you have the time——'

'Right, I 'll do so with pleasure. But still I don't see what this book 's got to do with these two poor women.'

'What 's it got to do with them? A great deal. Firstly' (Evpsychyi Afrikanovich ticked off the fat hairy forefinger of his left hand): '"It is the duty of a police sergeant to take the greatest care that all the people go to the Church of God, without, however, compelling them by force to remain there. . . ." I ask you, does she go—what 's her name; Manuilikha, isn't it? . . . Does she ever go to church?'

I was silent, surprised by the unexpected turn of his speech. He gave me a look of triumph, and ticked off his second finger. 'Secondly: "False prophecies and prognostications are everywhere forbidden. . . ." Do you notice that? Then, thirdly: "It is illegal to profess to be a sorcerer or a magician, or to employ similar deceptions." What do you say to that? And suppose all this becomes known, or gets round to the authorities by some back way, who has to pay for it? I do. Who gets sacked from the service? I do. Now you see what a business it is.'

He sat down in his chair again. His raised eyes wandered absently over the walls of the room and his fingers drummed loudly on the table.

'Well, what if I ask you, Evpsychyi Afrikanovich,' I began once more in a gentle voice. 'Of course I know your duties are complicated and troublesome, but you 've got a heart, I know, a heart of gold. What will it cost you to promise me not to touch these women?'

The sergeant's eyes suddenly stopped, over my head.

'That 's a nice little gun you 've got,' he said carelessly, still drumming his fingers. 'A splendid little gun. Last time I came to see you and you were out, I admired it all the while. A splendid gun!'

'Yes, it 's not a bad gun,' I agreed. 'It 's an old pattern, made by Gastin-Rennet; but last year I had it converted into a hammerless. You just look at the barrels.'

'Yes, yes . . . it was the barrels I admired most. . . . A magnificent piece of work. I 'd call it a perfect treasure.'

Our eyes met, and I saw the trace of a meaning smile flickering in the corner of the sergeant's lips. I rose from my seat, took the gun off the wall and approached Evpsychyi Afrikanovich with it.

'The Circassians have an admirable custom,' I said courteously, 'of presenting a guest with anything that he praises. Though we are not Circassians, Evpsychyi Afrikanovich, I entreat you to accept this from me as a memento.'

For appearance' sake the sergeant blushed.

'My goodness, what a beauty! No, no. . . . That custom is far too generous.'

However, I did not have to entreat him long. The sergeant accepted the gun, carefully put it between his knees and with a clean handkerchief lovingly wiped away the dust that had settled on the lock; and I was rather mollified when I saw that the gun had at least passed into the hands of an expert and an *amateur*. Almost immediately Evpsychyi Afrikanovich got up and began to hurry away.

'Business won't wait, and here I 've been gossiping with you,' he said, noisily banging on the floor with his reluctant goloshes. 'When you happen to come our way, you 'll be most welcome.'

'Well, what about Manuilikha, my dear Authority ?' I reminded him delicately.

'We 'll see, we 'll see, ...' Evpsychyi Afrikanovich vaguely muttered. 'There was something else I wanted to ask you. . . . Your radishes are magnificent. . . .'

'I grew them myself.'

'Mag-nificent radishes ! You know, my wife is terribly partial to garden-stuff. So, you know, one little bundle. . . .'

'With the greatest pleasure, Evpsychyi Afrikanovich. I consider it an obligation. . . . This very day I 'll send a basket by messenger. Let me send some butter as well. . . . My butter 's quite a special thing.'

'Well, butter too, . . .' the sergeant graciously permitted. 'And you can tip those women the wink that I shan't touch them for the time being. But you 'd better let them know '—he raised his voice suddenly—'that they can't settle *me* with a "Thank you." . . . Now, I wish you good-bye. Once more, *merci* for the present and the entertainment.'

He clicked his heels together like a soldier, and walked to his carriage with the ponderous gait of a full-fed, important person. By his carriage were already gathered the village policeman, the mayor and Yarmola, in respectful attitudes, with their heads bare.

IX

Evpsychyi Afrikanovich kept his word and left the people of the forest hut in peace indefinitely. But my relations with Olyessia suffered an acute and curious change. Not a trace of her old naïve and confident kindness remained in her attitude to me, nor any of the old animation wherein the coquetry of a beautiful girl so beautifully blended with the playful wantonness of a child. An awkward constraint beyond which we could not pass began to appear in our conversation. . . . With an instant timidity Olyessia avoided the lively themes which used to give such boundless scope to our curiosity.

In my presence she gave herself up to her work in a strained, stern, business-like way; but I often noticed that in the middle of her work her hands would suddenly drop weakly on her knees, and her eyes be fixed, vague and immovable, downwards upon the floor. And when at such a moment I called her by name, 'Olyessia,' or put some question to her, she shivered and turned her face slowly towards me: in it was reflected fright and the effort to understand the meaning of my words. Sometimes it seemed to me that she was burdened and embarrassed by my company, but I could not reconcile that with the deep interest that every remark and phrase of mine used to arouse in her only a few days ago. I could only think that Olyessia was unwilling to forgive my patronage in the affair with the sergeant, which so revolted her independent nature. But this solution did not satisfy me either, and I still asked myself from whence did this simple girl, who had grown up in the midst of the forest, derive her inordinately sensitive pride ?

All this demanded explanations ; but Olyessia avoided every favourable occasion for frank conversation. Our evening walks came to an end. In vain I cast eloquent imploring glances at Olyessia each day, when I was on the point of leaving ; she made as though she did not understand their meaning, and in spite of the old woman's deafness, her presence disturbed me.

At times I revolted against my own weakness and the habit which now drew me every day to Olyessia. I myself did not suspect with what subtle, strong, invisible threads my heart was bound to this fascinating, incomprehensible girl. As yet I had no thought of love ; but I was already living through a disturbing period of unconscious anticipation, full of vague and oppressive sadnesses. Wherever I was, with whatever I tried to amuse myself, my every thought was occupied with the image of Olyessia, my whole being craved for her, and each separate memory of her most insignificant words, her gestures and her smiles, contracted my heart with a sweet and gentle pain. But evening came and I sat long beside her on a low rickety little bench, to my grief finding myself every time more timid, more awkward and foolish.

Once I passed a whole day thus at Olyessia's side. I had begun to feel unwell from the morning onward, though I could not clearly define wherein my sickness consisted. It grew worse towards evening. My head grew heavy; I felt a dull incessant pain in the crown of my head, exactly as though some one were pressing down upon it with a soft, strong hand. My mouth was parched, and an idle, languid weakness poured over my whole body. My eyes pained me just as though I had been staring fixedly, close to a glimmering point.

As I was returning late in the evening, midway I was suddenly seized and shaken by a tempestuous chill. I could hardly see the way as I went on; I was almost unconscious of where I was going; I reeled like a drunken man, and my jaws beat out a quick loud tattoo, each against the other.

Till this day I do not know who brought me into the house. For exactly six days I was stricken by a terrible racking Polyessian fever. During the day the sickness seemed to abate, and consciousness returned to me. Then, utterly exhausted by the disease, I could hardly walk across the room, such was the pain and weakness of my knees; at each stronger movement the blood rushed in a hot wave to my head, and covered everything before my eyes with darkness.

In the evening, and usually at about seven o'clock, the approach of the disease overwhelmed me like a storm, and on my bed I passed a terrible, century-long night, now shaking with cold beneath the blankets, now blazing with intolerable heat. Hardly had I been touched by a drowsy slumber, when strange, grotesque, painfully motley dreams began to play with my inflamed brain. Every dream was filled with tiny microscopic details, which piled up and clutched each at the other in ugly chaos. Now I seemed to be unpacking some boxes, coloured with stripes and of fantastic form, taking small ones out of the big, and from the small still smaller. I could not by any means interrupt the unending labour, although it had long been disgusting to me. Then there flashed before my eyes with stupefying speed long bright stripes from the wallpaper, and with amazing distinctness I saw on them, instead of patterns, whole garlands of human faces—beautiful, kind, and smiling, then horribly grimacing, thrusting out their tongues, showing their teeth, and rolling their eyes. Then I entered into a confused and extraordinarily complicated abstract dispute with Yarmola. Every minute the arguments which we brought up against each other became subtler and more profound: separate words and even individual letters of words suddenly took on a mysterious and unfathomable meaning, and at the same time I was seized by a revolting terror of the unknown, unnatural force that wound out one monstrous sophism after another outof my brain, and would not let me break off the dispute which had long been loathsome to me. . . .

It was like a seething whirlwind of human and animal figures, landscapes, things of the most wonderful forms and colours, words and phrases whose meaning was apprehended by every sense. . . . But the strange thing was that I never lost sight of a bright regular circle reflected on to the ceiling by the lamp with the scorched green shade. And somehow I knew that within the indistinct line of that quiet circle was concealed a silent, monotonous, mysterious, terrible life, yet more awful and oppressive than the mad chaos of my dreams.

Then I awoke, or more truly did not awake, but suddenly forced myself to sit up. Consciousness almost returned to me. I understood that I was lying in bed, that I was ill, that I had just been in delirium, but the bright circle on the ceiling still terrified me by its hidden, ominous menace. With weak hands I slowly reached for the watch, looked at it, and saw with melancholy perplexity that all the endless sequence of my ghastly dreams had taken no longer than two or three minutes. 'My God, will the dawn ever come?' I thought in despair, tossing my head over the hot pillows and feeling my short heavy breathing burn my lips. . . . But again a slight drowsiness possessed me, and again my brain became the sport of a motley nightmare, and again within two minutes I woke, racked by a mortal anguish.

In six days my vigorous constitution, aided by quinine and an infusion of buckthorn, overcame my disease. I rose from my bed completely crushed, with difficulty standing upright on my legs. But my convalescence passed with eager quickness. In my head, weary with six days' feverish delirium, I felt now an idle, pleasant absence of any thought at all. My appetite returned with double force, and hourly my body gathered strength, in each moment imbibing its particle of health and of the joy of life. And with that a new and stronger craving came upon me for the forest and the lonely, tumble-down hut. But my nerves had not yet recovered, and every time that I called up Olyessia's face and voice in my memory, I wanted to cry.

X

ONLY five more days had passed, when I was so much recovered that I reached the chicken-legged hut on foot without the least fatigue. As I stepped on the threshold my heart palpitated with breathless fear. I had not seen Olyessia for almost two weeks, and I now perceived how near and dear she was to me. Holding the latch of the door, I waited some seconds, breathing with difficulty. In my irresolution I even shut my eyes for some time before I could push the door open. . . .

It is always impossible to analyse impressions like those which followed my entrance. . . . Can one remember the words uttered in the first moment of meeting between a mother and son, husband and wife, or lover and lover? The simplest, most ordinary, even ridiculous words are said, if they were put down exactly upon paper. But each word is opportune and infinitely dear because it is uttered by the dearest voice in all the world.

I remember—very clearly I remember—only one thing: Olyessia's beautiful pale face turned quickly towards me, and on that beautiful face, so new to me, were in one second reflected, in changing succession, perplexity, fear, anxiety, and a tender radiant smile of love. . . . The old woman was mumbling something, clattering round me, but I did not hear her greetings. Olyessia's voice reached me like a sweet music:

'What has been the matter with you? You 've been ill? Ah, how thin you 've grown, my poor darling!'

For a long while I could make no answer, and we stood silent face to face, clasping hands and looking straight into the depths of each other's eyes, happily. Those few silent seconds I have always considered the happiest in my life: never, never before or since, have I tasted such pure, complete, all-absorbing ecstasy. And how much I read in Olyessia's big dark eyes!—the excitement of the meeting, reproach for my long absence, and a passionate declaration of love. In that look I felt that Olyessia gave me her whole being joyfully without doubt or reservation.

She was the first to break the spell, pointing to Manuilikha with a slow movement of her eyelids. We sat down side by side, and Olyessia began to ask me anxiously for the details of my illness, the medicines I had taken, what the doctor had said and thought—he came twice to see me from the little town; she made me tell about the doctor time after time, and I could catch a fleeting, sarcastic smile on her lips.

'Oh, why didn't I know that you were ill!' she exclaimed with impatient regret. 'I would have set you on your feet again in a single day.

. . . How can they be trusted, when they don't understand anything at all, nothing at all? Why didn't you send for me?'

I was at a loss for an answer.

'You see, Olyessia . . . it happened so suddenly . . . besides, I was afraid to trouble you. Towards the end you had become strange towards me, as though you were angry with me, or bored. . . . Olyessia,' I added, lowering my voice, 'we 've got ever so much to say to each other, ever so much . . . just we two . . . you understand?'

She quietly cast down her eyes in token of consent, and then whispered quickly, looking round timidly at her grandmother:

'Yes. . . . I want to, as well . . . later . . . wait——'

As soon as the sun began to set, Olyessia began to urge me to go home.

'Make haste, be quick and get ready,' she said, pulling my hand from the bench. 'If the damp catches you now, the fever will be on you again, immediately.'

'Where are you going, Olyessia?' Manuilikha asked suddenly, seeing that her granddaughter had thrown a large grey shawl hurriedly over her head.

'I 'm going part of the way with him,' answered Olyessia.

She said the words with indifference, looking not at her grandmother but at the window; but in her voice I could detect an almost imperceptible note of irritation.

'You 're really going ?' the old woman once more asked, meaningly.

Olyessia's eyes flashed, and she stared steadily into Manuilikha's face.

'Yes, I am going,' she replied proudly. 'We talked it out and talked it out long ago. . . . It 's my affair, and my own responsibility.'

'Ah, you——' the old woman exclaimed in reproach and annoyance. She wanted to add more, but only waved her hand and dragged her trembling legs away into the corner, and began to busy herself with a basket, groaning.

I understood that the brief unpleasant conversation which I had just witnessed was a continuation of a long series of mutual quarrels and bursts of anger. As I walked to the forest at Olyessia's side, I asked her :

'Granny doesn't want you to go for a walk with me, does she ?'

Olyessia shrugged her shoulders in vexation.

'Please, don't take any notice of it. . . . No, she doesn't like it. . . . Surely I 'm free to do as I like ?'

Suddenly I conceived an irresistible desire to reproach Olyessia with her former sternness.

'But you could have done it before my illness as well. . . . Only then you didn't want to be alone with me. . . . I thought, every evening I thought, perhaps you would come with me again. But you used to pay no attention ; you were so unresponsive, and cross. . . . How you tormented me, Olyessia ! . . .'

'Don't, darling. . . . Forget it, . . .'

Olyessia entreated with a tender apology in her voice.

'No, I 'm not saying it to blame you. It just slipped out. Now, I understand why it was. . . . But before—it 's funny to talk about it even now—I thought you were offended because of the sergeant. The thought made me terribly sad. I couldn't help thinking that you considered me so remote and foreign to you, that you found it hard to accept a simple kindness from me. . . . It was very bitter to me. . . . I never even suspected that granny was the cause of it all, Olyessia.'

Olyessia's face suddenly flamed bright red.

'But it wasn't granny at all. . . . It was me. I didn't want it, myself,' she exclaimed with a passionate challenge.

'But why didn't you want it, Olyessia, why?' I asked. My voice broke for agitation, and I caught her by the hand and made her stop. We were just in the middle of a long narrow path, straight as an arrow through the forest. On either side we were surrounded by tall slender pines, that formed a gigantic corridor, receding into the distance, vaulted with fragrant interwoven branches. The bare peeled trunks were tinged with the purple glow of the burnt-out red of the evening sky.

'Tell me why, Olyessia, why?' I whispered again, pressing her hand closer and closer.

'I could not . . . I was afraid,' Olyessia said so low that I could hardly hear. 'I thought it was possible to escape one's destiny. . . . But, now . . . now.'

Her breath failed her, as though there were no air ; and suddenly her hands twined quick and vehement about my neck, and my lips were sweetly burnt by Olyessia's quick trembling whisper:

'But it 's all the same, now . . . all the same! . . . Because I love you, my dear, my joy, my beloved!'

She pressed closer and closer to me, and I could feel how her strong, vigorous, fervent body pulsed beneath my hands, how quickly her heart beat against my chest. Her passionate kisses poured like intoxicating wine into my head, still weak with disease, and I began to lose my hold upon myself.

'Olyessia, for God's sake, don't . . . leave me,' I said, trying to unclasp her hands. 'Now I am afraid. . . . I 'm afraid of myself. . . Let me go, Olyessia.'

She raised her head. Her face was all lighted with a slow, languid smile.

'Don't be afraid, my darling,' she said with an indescribable expression of tender passion and touching fearlessness. 'I shall never reproach you, never be jealous of any one. . . . Tell me only, do you love me?'

'I love you, Olyessia. I loved you long ago, and I love you passionately. But . . . don't kiss me any more. . . . I grow weak, my head swims, I can't answer for myself. . . .'

Her lips were once more pressed to mine in a

long, painful sweetness. I did not hear, rather I divined her words.

'Then don't be afraid. Don't think of anything besides. . . . To-day is ours; no one can take it from us.'

And the whole night melted into a magical fairy tale. The moon rose, and its radiance poured fantastically in motley and mysterious colours over the forest. It lay amid the darkness in pale blue stains upon the gnarled tree-trunks, on the bent branches and the soft carpet of moss. The high birch-trunks showed clear and keenly white, and it seemed that a silvery transparent veil of gauze had been thrown over the thin leaves. In places the light could by no means penetrate the thick canopy of pine branches. There was complete, impenetrable darkness, save only that in the middle a ray slipped in unknown from somewhere and suddenly shone brightly on a long row of trees, casting a straight narrow path on the earth, as bright and trim and beautiful as a path fashioned by fairies for the triumphant procession of Oberon and Titania. And we walked with our arms enlocked through this vivid, smiling fairy-tale, without a single word, under the weight of our happiness and the dreadful silence of the night.

'Darling, I 've forgotten quite that you must hurry home,' Olyessia suddenly remembered. 'What a wicked girl I am! You 're only just recovering from your illness and I 've kept you all this while in the forest.'

I kissed her, and threw back the shawl from her thick dark hair, and asked her in the softest whisper, bending to her ear:

'You don't regret it, Olyessia? You don't repent?'

She shook her head slowly.

'No, no. . . . Come what may, I shan't regret. . . . I am so happy!'

'Is something bound to happen, then?'

There appeared in her eyes a flash of the mystical terror I had grown to recognise.

'Yes, it is certain. You remember I told you about the queen of clubs. That queen of clubs is me, myself; the misfortune that the cards told of will happen to me. . . . You know I thought of asking you not to come and see us any more. But then you fell ill, and I never saw you for nearly a fortnight. . . . I was so anxious and sad for you that I felt I could have given the whole world to be with you, just one little minute. Then I thought that I would not give up my happiness, whatever should come of it. . . .'

'It's true, Olyessia. That's how it was with me, too,' I said, touching her forehead with my lips. 'I never knew that I loved you until I parted from you. It seems that man was right who said that parting to love is like wind to a fire: it blows out a small one, and makes a large one blaze.'

'What did you say? Say it again, again, please.' Olyessia was interested.

I repeated the words again. I do not know

whose they are. Olyessia mused over them, and I could see by the movement of her lips that she was saying the words over to herself.

I looked closely into her pale face, thrown back, her large black eyes with glimmering bright lights within them from the moon ; and with a sudden chill a vague foreboding of imminent calamity crept into my soul.

XI

THE naïve enchanting tale of our love lasted for nearly a month. To this day there live with undiminished potency in my soul Olyessia's beautiful face and those blazing twilights, those dewy mornings fragrant with lilies and honey, full of vigorous freshness and the sonorous noise of birds, those hot, languid, idle days of June. In that time neither weariness, nor fatigue, nor my eternal passion for a wandering life ever touched my soul. I was a pagan god or a strong, young animal, delighting in the light and warmth and conscious joy of life, and in calm, pure, sensuous love.

After my recovery old Manuilikha became so intolerably snappish, met me with such undisguised malice, and, while I was sitting in the hut, moved the pots on the stove with such noisy exasperation, that Olyessia and I preferred to meet in the forest every evening. . . . And the stately green beauty of the pine-forest was the precious setting which adorned our tranquil love.

Every day with deeper and deeper wonder I discovered that Olyessia, the child of the forest who could not even read, showed in many things of life a delicate sensitiveness and a peculiar native refinement. There are always horrible sides to love, in its direct and coarser meaning, which are a torment and a shame to nervous artistic natures. But Olyessia could avoid them with such naïve chastity that our love was never once spoiled by a single ugly thought, or one moment of cynicism.

Meanwhile the time of my departure was approaching. To tell the truth, all my official business at Perebrod was already at an end; but I had deliberately delayed my return to town. I had not yet breathed a word of this to Olyessia, for I was afraid even to imagine to myself how she would receive the news that I must go away. Habit had taken roots too deep in me. To see Olyessia every day, to hear her dear voice and musical laughter, to feel the tender beauty of her caresses, had come to be more than a necessity for me. On the rare days when stress of weather prevented us from meeting I felt exactly as though I had been lost, and deprived of what was chief and all-important in my life. Every occupation was tedious and useless to me, and my whole being craved for the forest, the warmth and the light, and Olyessia's dear familiar face.

The idea of marrying Olyessia entered my head more and more insistently. At first it had only presented itself to me but rarely as a possible, and in extremities an honest, issue to our relationship. Only one thing alarmed and checked me. I dared not even imagine to myself what Olyessia would be like, fashionably dressed, chatting to the wives of my colleagues in the drawing-room, snatched away from the fascinating setting of the old forest, full of legends and mysterious powers.

But the nearer came the time for me to depart, the greater was the anguish and horror of loneliness which possessed me. My resolution to marry grew daily stronger in my soul, and finally I could no longer see it as a bold defiance of society. 'Decent, well-educated men marry dressmakers and servant-maids,' I consoled myself, 'and they live happily together, and to the day of their death they thank the fate which urged them to this resolution. Shall I be unhappier than the others?'

Once in mid-June, towards evening, I was waiting for Olyessia, according to my habit, at the turn of a narrow forest path among the flowering whitethorn bushes. When she was far in the distance I made out the easy, quick sound of her steps.

'How are you, my darling?' Olyessia said, embracing me and breathing heavily. 'Have I kept you waiting too long? . . . It was so hard to get away at the last. . . . Fighting with granny all the while.'

'Isn't she reconciled yet?'

'Never! She says to me: "He'll ruin you. . . . He'll play with you at his pleasure and then desert you. . . . He doesn't love you at all——"'

'So that's what she says about me?'

'Yes, darling, about you. . . . But I don't believe a single word of it all the same. . . .'

'Does she know everything?'

'I couldn't say for sure. . . . But I believe she knows. . . . I've never spoken to her about it—she guesses. But what's the good of thinking about that. . . . Come.'

She plucked a twig of whitethorn with a superb spray of blossom and thrust it into her hair. We walked slowly along the path which showed faintly rosy beneath the evening sun.

The night before I had decided that I would speak out at all costs this evening. But a strange timidity lay like a weight upon my tongue. 'If I tell Olyessia that I am going away and going to marry her,' I thought, 'will she not think that my proposal is only made to soothe the pain of the first wound? . . . But I'll begin the moment we reach that maple with the peeled trunk,' I fixed in my mind. We were already on a level with the maple. Pale with agitation I had begun to draw a deep breath to begin to speak, when my courage suddenly failed, and ended in a nervous painful beating of my heart and a chill on my lips. 'Twenty-seven is my number,' I thought a few moments later. 'I'll count up to twenty-seven, and then! . . .' I began to count to myself, but when I reached twenty-seven I felt that the resolution had not yet matured in me. 'No,' I said to myself, 'I'd better go on counting to sixty . . . that will make just a minute, and then without fail, without fail——'

'What's the matter with you to-day?' Olyessia suddenly asked. 'You're thinking of something unpleasant. What has happened to you?'

Then I began to speak, but with a tone repugnant to myself, with an assumed unnatural carelessness, just as though it were a trifling affair.

'Yes, it really is rather unpleasant. . . . You have guessed it, Olyessia. . . . You see, my service here is finished, and the authorities have summoned me back to town.'

I took a quick side-glance at Olyessia. The colour died away from her face and her lips quivered. She said not a word in reply. Some minutes I walked in silence by her side. The grasshoppers chattered noisily in the grass, and the strained monotonous note of a corncrake sounded somewhere afar.

'Of course you understand, yourself, Olyessia,' I again began, 'that it's no good my staying here, besides there's nowhere to stay. . . . And I can't neglect my duty——'

'No . . . why . . . what's the good of talking?' Olyessia said, in a voice outwardly calm, but so deep and lifeless that terror seized me. 'If it's your duty, of course . . . you must go——'

She stopped by the tree and leaned against the trunk, her face utterly pale, her hands hanging limply by her body, a poignant pitiful smile on her lips. Her pallor frightened me. I rushed to her and pressed her hands vehemently.

'What's the matter, Olyessia . . . darling!'

'Nothing . . . forgive me. . . . It will pass

—now. . . . My head is dizzy.' She controlled herself with an effort and went on, leaving her hand in mine.

'You 're thinking ill of me, Olyessia,' I said reproachfully. 'You should be ashamed. Do you think, as well, that I could cast you off and leave you ? No, my darling. That 's why I began this conversation—so that you should go this very day to your grandmother and tell her you will be my wife.'

Quite contrary to my expectation, Olyessia showed hardly a trace of surprise at my words.

'Your wife ? ' She shook her head slowly and sadly. 'No, it 's impossible, Vanichka dear.'

'Why, Olyessia ? Why ? '

'No, no. . . . You can see yourself, it 's funny to think of it even. What kind of wife could I be for you ? You are a gentleman, clever, educated—and I ? I can't even read. I don't know how to behave. You will be ashamed to be my husband. . . .'

'What nonsense, Olyessia,' I replied fervently. 'In six months you won't know yourself. You don't even suspect the natural wit and genius for observation you have in you. We 'll read all sorts of good books together ; we 'll make friends with decent, clever people ; we 'll see the whole wide world together, Olyessia. We 'll go together arm in arm just like we are now until old age, to the grave itself ; and I shan't be ashamed of you, but proud and grateful. . . .'

Olyessia answered my passionate speech with a grateful clasp of the hand, but she persisted :

'That 's not everything. . . . Perhaps you don't know, yet. . . . I never told you. . . . I haven't a father. . . . I 'm illegitimate. . . .'

'Don't, Olyessia. . . . That 's the last thing I care about. What have I got to do with your family, when you yourself are more precious to me than my father and mother, than the whole world even? No, this is all trifling—just excuses! . . .'

Olyessia pressed her shoulder against mine with a gentle submissive caress.

'Darling! . . . You 'd better not have begun to talk at all. . . . You are young, free. . . . Would I ever dare to tie you hand and foot for all your life? . . . What if you fall in love with another woman afterwards? Then you will despise me, and curse the day and hour when I agreed to marry you. Don't be angry, darling!' she cried out in entreaty, seeing by my face that the words had offended me, 'I don't want to hurt you. . . . I 'm only thinking of your happiness. And you 've forgotten granny. Well, ask yourself, could I leave her alone?'

'Why . . . she 'll come with us, too.' (I confess the idea of granny made me uneasy.) 'And even if she didn't want to live with us . . . there are houses in every town . . . called almshouses, where such old women are given rest, and carefully looked after.'

'No, what are you saying? She will never go away from the forest. She is afraid of people.'

'Well, think of something better yourself, Olyessia. You must choose between me and granny. But I tell you this one thing—that life will be hideous to me without you.'

'You darling!' Olyessia said with profound tenderness. 'Just for those words I am grateful. . . . You have warmed my heart. . . . But still I shan't marry you. . . . I rather go with you without being married, if you don't send me away. . . . But don't be in a hurry, please don't hurry me. Give me a day or two. I'll think it over well. . . . Besides, I must speak to granny, as well.'

'Tell me, Olyessia,' I asked, for the shadow of a new thought was upon my mind. 'Perhaps you are still . . . afraid of the church?'

Perhaps I should have begun with this question. Almost every day I used to quarrel with Olyessia over it, trying to shake her belief in the imaginary curse that hung over her family for the possession of magic powers. There is something of the preacher essential in every Russian intellectual. It is in our blood; it has been instilled by the whole of Russian literature in the last generations. Who could say but, if Olyessia had had a profound belief, and strictly observed the fasts, and never missed a single service, it is quite possible I would have begun to speak ironically (but only a little, for I was always a believer myself) of her piety and to develop a critical curiosity of mind in her. But with a firm, naïve conviction she professed her communion with the powers of darkness, and her estrangement from God, of whom she was afraid to speak.

In vain I tried to shake Olyessia's superstition. All my logical arguments, all my mockery, sometimes rude and wicked, were broken against her submissive confidence in her mysterious, fatal vocation.

'You 're afraid of the church, Olyessia?' I repeated.

She bent her head in silence.

'You think God will not accept you?' I continued with growing passion. 'That He will not have mercy on you; He who, though He commands millions of angels, yet came down to earth and suffered a horrible infamous death for the salvation of all men? He who did not disdain the repentance of the worst woman, and promised a highway murderer that on that very day he would sit together with Him in Paradise?'

This interpretation of mine was already familiar to Olyessia; but this time she did not even listen to me. With a quick movement she took off her shawl, rolled it up and flung it in my face. A struggle began. I tried to snatch her nosegay of whitethorn away. She resisted, fell on the ground and dragged me down with her, laughing joyfully and holding out to me her darling lips, moist and opened by her quick breathing. . . .

Late at night, when we had said good-bye and were already a good distance away from each other, I suddenly heard Olyessia's voice behind me: 'Vanichka! Wait a moment. . . . I want to tell you something.'

I turned and went to meet her. Olyessia quickly ran up to me. Already the thin notched silver sickle of the young moon stood in the sky, and by its light I saw that Olyessia's eyes were full of big brimming tears.

'What is it, Olyessia?' I asked anxiously.

She seized my hands and began to kiss them in turn.

'Darling . . . how sweet you are! How good you are!' she said with a trembling voice. 'I was just walking and thinking how much you love me. . . . You see I want awfully to do something that you would like very, very much.'

'Olyessia . . . my precious girl, be calm——'

'Tell me,' she continued, 'would you be very glad if I went to church some time? Tell me the truth, the real truth.'

I was thinking. A superstitious thought suddenly crossed my mind that some misfortune would come of it.

'Why don't you answer? Tell me quickly; would you be glad, or is it all the same to you?'

'How can I say, Olyessia?' I began doubtfully. 'Well, yes. . . . I would be glad. I've said many times that a man may disbelieve, doubt, even laugh finally. But a woman . . . a woman must be religious without any sophistication. I always feel something touching, feminine, beautiful in the simple tender confidence with which a woman surrenders herself to the protection of God.'

I was silent; neither did Olyessia make any answer, but nestled her head in my bosom.

'Why did you ask me this?' I was curious.

She started suddenly.

'Nothing. . . . I just asked. . . . Don't take any notice. Now, good-bye, darling. Come to-morrow.'

She disappeared. I stood still for a long while, looking into the darkness, listening eagerly to the quick steps going away from me. A sudden dread foreboding seized me. I had an irresistible desire to run after Olyessia, to take hold of her and ask, implore, demand, if need be, that she should not go to church. But I checked the sudden impulse, and I remember that as I went my way I even said aloud:

'It seems to me, my dear Vanichka, that the superstition 's touched you as well.'

My God, why did I not listen then to the dim voice of the heart, which—I now believe it implicitly—never errs in its momentary mysterious presentiments?

XII

THE day after this meeting was Whitsuntide, which that year fell on the day of the great martyr Timothy, when, according to the folk legends, the omens of a bad harvest befall. Ecclesiastically the village of Perebrod was considered auxiliary; that is to say, that though there was a church there it had no priest of its own. On rare occasions, in fast time and on the great festivals, it was served by the priest of the village of Volchye.

That day my official duties took me to the neighbouring town, and I set off thither on horseback about eight o'clock, in the chill of the morning. A good time before I had bought a small cob for doing my rounds, a beast six or seven years old, which came from the rough local breed, but had been carefully looked after and made a pet of by the former owner, the district surveyor. The horse's name was Taranchik. I became greatly attached to the dear beast, with its strong, thin, chiselled legs, with its shaggy mane, from beneath which peeped fiery eyes, with firm, close-pressed lips. Its colour was rare and curious, a grey mouse-colour all over the body save for a piebald rump.

I had to pass right through the village. The

big green that ran from the church to the inn was completely covered by long rows of carts in which the peasants of the neighbouring villages had come with their wives and children for the holiday—from Volocha, Zoulnya, and Pechalovka. People were roaming about among the carts. Notwithstanding the early hour and the strict regulations one could already see drunken people among them. (On holidays and at night Shroul, the former innkeeper, sold vodka on the quiet.) The morning was windless and close. The air was sultry and the day promised to be insufferably hot. There was not a single cloud to be seen in the glowing sky, which looked exactly as though it were covered with a silver dust.

When I had done all my business in the little town I had a light hasty meal of pike, stuffed and cooked in the Jewish fashion, washed down with some very inferior muddy beer, and set out for home. As I passed by the smithy I recollected that Taranchik's off fore-shoe had been loose for some time, and I stopped to have him shod. That took me another hour and a half, so that by the time I was nearing Perebrod it was already between four and five o'clock in the afternoon.

The whole square was packed with drunken, shouting people. The yard and porch of the inn were literally choked by jostling, pushing customers; the Perebrod men were mixed up with strangers, sitting on the grass and in the shade of the carts. Everywhere were heads thrown back and lifted bottles. There was not a single man sober; and the general intoxication had reached the point at which the peasant begins noisily boasting and exaggerating his own drunkenness, and all his movements acquire a feeble, ponderous freedom, when, for instance, in order to nod 'yes' he bows his whole body down, bends his knees, and, suddenly losing his balance completely, draws back helplessly. The children were pushing and screaming in the same place beneath the horses' legs, while the horses munched their hay unconcerned. Elsewhere, a woman who could hardly stand on her feet herself dragged her reluctant husband, foully drunk, home by the sleeve. . . . In the shade of a fence about twenty men and women peasants were pressed close round a blind harpist, whose tremulous, snuffling tenor, accompanied by the monotonous, jingling drone of his instrument, rose sharp above the dull murmur of the crowd. At a distance I could hear the familiar words of the Little Russian song:

> 'Oh, there rose the star, the evening star,
> And stood over Pochah monastery.
> Oh, there came out the Turkish troops
> Like unto a black cloud.'

This song goes on to tell how the Turks, failing in their attack upon the Pochayev monastery, resolved to take it by cunning. With this end they sent, as it were a gift to the monastery, a huge candle filled with gunpowder. The candle was dragged by twelve yoke of oxen, and the delighted monks were eager to light it before the icon of the Virgin ; but God did not allow the wicked design to be accomplished.

‘ And the elder dreamt a dream
That he should not take the candle,
But bear it away to the open field,
And hew it down with an axe.’

And the monks :

‘ Took it into the open field,
And began to chop it,
Oh, then bullets and balls began
To scatter on every side.’

It seemed that the insufferably hot air was wholly saturated with a disgusting smell, compounded of vodka dregs, onions, sheep-skins, strong shag, and the vapours of dirty human bodies. As I made my way through the people, hardly holding in Taranchik who tossed his head continually, I could not help noticing that unceremonious, curious, and hostile looks were bent on me from every side. Not a single man doffed his cap, which was quite unusual, but the noise grew still at my approach. Suddenly from the very middle of the crowd came a hoarse, drunken shout which I could not clearly distinguish ; but it was answered by a restrained giggle. A frightened woman's voice began to rebuke the brawler.

‘ Hush, you fool. . . . What are you shouting for ? He 'll hear you——’

‘ What if he does hear ? ’ the peasant replied tauntingly. ‘ What the hell 's he got to do with me ? Is he an official ? He 's only in the forest with his——'

A long, filthy, horrible phrase hung in the air, with a burst of frantic, roaring laughter. I quickly turned my horse round, and seized the handle of my whip convulsively, overwhelmed by the mad fury which sees nothing, thinks of nothing, and is afraid of nothing. In a flash, a strange, anxious, painful thought went through my mind : ' All this has happened once before in my life, many years ago. . . . The sun blazed just as it does now. . . . The whole of the big square was overflowing with a noisy, excited crowd just as it is now. . . . I turned back in a paroxysm of wild anger just in the same way. . . . But where was it ? When ? When ? ' I lowered my whip and madly galloped home.

Yarmola came out of the kitchen at his leisure, and said rudely, as he took my horse : ' The bailiff of the Marenov farm is sitting in your room.'

I had the fancy that he wanted to add something more that was important to me and painful too ; I even imagined that a fleeting expression of evil derision sped over his face. Intentionally I stopped dead in the doorway and gave Yarmola a look of challenge, but without looking at me he was already dragging the horse away by the rein. The horse's head was stretched forward, and it stepped delicately.

In my room I found the agent of the neighbouring estate, Nikita Nazarich Mishtchenko. He was dressed in a grey jacket with large ginger checks, in narrow cornflower blue trousers, and a fiery red necktie. There was a deep parting down the middle of his hair, which shone with pomade, and from the whole of him exuded the scent of Persian lilac. When he saw me he jumped up from his chair and began to curtsy, not bowing, but somehow breaking at the waist, and at the same time unsheathing the pale gums of both his jaws.

'Extremely delighted to have the honour,' Nikita Nazarich jabbered courteously. 'Very glad indeed to see you. I 've been waiting for you here ever since the service. I hadn't seen you for so long that I was bored, and missed you very much. Why is it you never look us up? The girls in Stiepany laugh at you nowadays.'

Suddenly he was seized by an instantaneous recollection, and broke out into an irresistible giggle.

'What fun it was to-day!' he cried out, choking and chuckling. 'Ha, ha, ha, ha. . . . I fairly split my sides with laughing.'

'What do you mean? What fun?' I asked without troubling to conceal my annoyance.

'There was a row after service,' Nikita Nazarich continued, punctuating his words with volleys of laughter. 'The Perebrod girls. . . . No, by God, I really can't. . . . The Perebrod girls caught a witch in the market-place here. Of course, it 's only their peasant ignorance that makes them think she 's a witch. . . . But they did give her a thrashing! They were going to tar her all over, but somehow she slipped from them and got away-——'

A ghastly surmise entered my head. I rushed towards the bailiff, and forgetting myself completely in my agitation, gripped him violently by the shoulders.

'What 's that you say ?' I cried in a furious voice. 'Stop your giggling, damn you ? Who 's this witch you 're talking about ?'

Instantly his laughing ceased, and he stared with his round, frightened eyes. . . .

'I . . . I . . . really don't know,' he began to stammer in confusion. 'I believe it was some one called Samoilikha . . . Manuilikha, was it ? . . . Yes, that 's it, the daughter of some one called Manuilikha. . . . The peasants were shouting something or other, but honestly I don't remember what it was.'

I made him tell me everything he had seen and heard in order. He told his tale absurdly, incoherently, confusing details, and every moment I interrupted him with impatient questions and exclamations, almost with abuse. I could understand very little from his story, and it was only two months later that I could piece together the real order of the vile happening from the words of an eyewitness, the wife of the forester of the Crown Lands, who was also present at Mass that day.

I had not been deceived by my foreboding. Olyessia had broken down her fears and come to church. Though she did not reach the church until the service was half done, and stopped in the entry, her arrival was instantly noticed by every peasant in church. All through the service the women were whispering to each other and glancing behind them.

However Olyessia had strength enough in herself to stand out the Mass right to the end. Perhaps she did not understand the real meaning of those hostile looks; perhaps she despised them out of pride. But when she came out of the church she could get no farther than the church fence before she was surrounded by a crowd of women, which grew larger and larger every minute, and pressed closer and closer upon Olyessia. At first they only examined the helpless girl in silence and without ceremony, while she looked everywhere about her in fright. Then there came a shower of rude insults, hard words, abuse, accompanied by roars of laughter; then all separate words disappeared into one general piercing women's shriek, wherein everything was confused and the nerves of the agitated crowd became more and more tightly strung. Several times Olyessia attempted to pass through this horrible living ring, but every time she was pushed back into the middle again. Suddenly the squeaking voice of some old hag shrieked from somewhere at the back of the crowd: 'Smear the slut with tar—tar the slut!' (Everybody knows that in Little Russia to smear with tar even the gates of the house where a girl lives is considered as a mark of the greatest, the most indelible, disgrace to her.) Almost the same second a pot of tar and a brush appeared over the heads of the raging furies, passed from hand to hand.

Then Olyessia, seized by a paroxysm of anger, horror and despair, rushed on the nearest of her tormentors with such impetuous force that she was thrown to the ground. Immediately a fight burst forth, and innumerable bodies were confused in one general shouting mass. But by some miracle Olyessia succeeded in slipping out from among the tangle, and rushed headlong down the road, without her shawl, her clothes torn to ribbons, through which in many places her naked body could be seen. Stones, vile abuse, laughter and shouts sped after her. . . . When she had run fifty paces Olyessia stopped, turned her pale, scratched, bleeding face to the crowd, and said so loud that each word could be heard all through the square: 'Very well. . . . You will remember this. You will weep your fill for this, all of you!'

The eyewitness of the happening told me afterwards that this threat was pronounced with such passionate hatred, in such a determined tone of prophecy, that for a moment the whole crowd was as it were benumbed; but only for a moment, because a fresh explosion of curses was heard immediately.

I say again that it was not till long after that I came to know many details of this story. I had neither strength nor patience to hear Mishtchenko's tale to the end. I suddenly remember that Yarmola had probably not had time yet to unsaddle my horse, and without a word to the astounded bailiff, I rushed out into the yard. Yarmola was still leading Taranchik along by the fence. I quickly slipped the bridle on, tightened thc girths, and raced away into the forest by circuitous paths in order to avoid having to pass through the drunken crowd again.

XIII

I CANNOT possibly describe my state during that wild gallop. There were moments when I utterly forgot where and why I was riding; only a dim consciousness remained that something irreparable had happened, something grotesque and horrible; a consciousness like the heavy, causeless anxiety which will possess a person in a feverish nightmare. And all the while strangely rang in my head, in time with the horse's hoof-beat, the snuffling, broken voice of the harpist:

'Oh, there came out the Turkish troops
Like unto a black cloud.'

When I reached the narrow footpath that led straight to Manuilikha's hut, I jumped off Taranchik and led him by the rein. By the edge of the saddle pads, and wherever the girths and bridle touched him, stood out white lumps of thick froth. From the violent heat of the day and the speed of my gallop, the blood roared in my head as though forced by some immense, unceasing pump.

I tied my horse to the wattle hedge and entered the hut. At first I thought that Olyessia was not there, and my heart and lips were chilled with fear; but a minute later I saw her lying on the bed with her face to the wall and her head hidden in the pillows. She did not even turn at the noise of the opening door.

Manuilikha was squatting on the floor by her side. When she saw me she rose with effort to her feet and shook her hand at me.

'Sh! Don't make a noise, curse you!' she said in a menacing whisper, coming close to me. She glanced with her cold, faded eyes straight into mine and hissed malignantly: 'Yes! You 've done that beautifully, my darling!'

'Look here, granny!' I answered sternly. 'This isn't the time to settle our account and abuse each other. What 's the matter with Olyessia?'

'Sh. . . . Sh! Olyessia 's lying there unconscious; that 's what 's the matter with Olyessia! If you hadn't poked your nose in where you had no business, and talked a pack of nonsense to the girl, nothing wrong would have happened. And I just looked on and indulged it, blind fool that I am. . . . But my heart scented misfortune. . . . It scented misfortune from the very first day when you broke into our house, almost by force. Do you mean to say that it wasn't you who persuaded her to go trailing off to church?' Suddenly the old woman looked at me with her face distorted with hatred. 'Wasn't it you, you cursed gentleman! Don't lie—don't put me off with your cunning tricks, you shameless hound! What did you go enticing her to church for?'

'I didn't entice her, granny. . . . I give you my word. She wanted to, herself.'

'Ah, my grief, my misfortune!' Manuilikha clasped her hands. 'She came running back from there—with no face left at all, and all her skirt in rags . . . without a shawl to her head. . . . She tells me how it happened . . . then she laughs, or cries. . . . Just possessed simply. . . . She lay on the bed . . . weeping all the while, and then I saw that she 'd fallen into a sleep, I thought. . . . And I was happy like an old fool. "She 'll sleep it all away now, for good," I thought. I saw her hand hanging down, and I thought I 'd better put it right, or it would swell. . . . I felt for the darling's hand and it was burning, blazing. . . . That meant the fever had begun. . . . For an hour she never stopped speaking, fast, and so pitifully. . . . She only stopped this very minute, a moment ago. . . . What have you done? What have you done to her?'

Suddenly her brown face writhed into a monstrous, disgusting grimace of weeping. Her lips tightened and drooped at the corners: all the muscles of her face stiffened and trembled, her eyelids lifted and wrinkled her forehead into deep folds, and from her eyes came a quick rain of big tears, big as peas. She held her head in her hands, and with her elbows on the table began to rock her whole body to and fro and to whine in a low, drawn-out voice.

'My little daught-er! My darling grand-daught-er! Oh, it is so hard for me, so bit-te-r!'

'Don't roar, you old fool!' I coarsely broke in on Manuilikha. 'You 'll wake her!'

The old woman kept silence, but with the same terrible contortion of her face she went on swinging to and fro, while the big tears splashed on to the table. . . . About ten minutes passed in this way. I sat by Manuilikha's side and anxiously listened to a fly knocking against the window-pane with a broken yet monotonous buzzing. . . .

'Granny!' suddenly a faint, barely audible voice came from Olyessia: 'Granny, who 's here?'

Manuilikha hastily hobbled to the bed, and straightway began to whine once more.

'Oh, my granddaughter, my own! Oh, it is so hard for me, so bit-t-e-r!'

'Ah, stop, granny, stop!' Olyessia said with complaining entreaty and suffering in her voice. 'Who 's sitting here?'

Cautiously, I approached the bed on tip-toe, with the awkward, guilty conscience of my own gross health which one always feels by a sick bed.

'It 's me, Olyessia,' I said, lowering my voice. 'I 've just come from the village on horseback. . . . I was in the town all the morning. . . . You 're ill, Olyessia?'

Without moving her face from the pillow, she stretched out her bare hand, as though she were feeling for something in the air. I understood the movement and took her hot hand into mine. Two huge blue marks, one on the wrist, the other above the elbow, stood out sharp on her tender white skin.

'My darling,' Olyessia began to speak slowly, with difficulty separating one word from another. 'I want . . . to look at you . . . but I cannot. . . . They 've maimed me. . . . All over, my whole body. . . . You remember. . . . You loved my face, so much. . . . You loved it, darling, didn't you ? . . . It made me so glad, always. . . . And now it will disgust you . . . even to look at me. . . . That is why . . . I do not want——'

'Forgive me, Olyessia ! ' I whispered, bending down to her ear.

Her burning hand pressed mine hard and held it long.

'But what are you saying ? Why should I forgive you, my darling ? Aren't you ashamed to think of it even ? How could it be your fault ? It 's all my own—stupid me. . . . Why did I go ? . . . No, my precious, don't blame yourself. . . .'

'Olyessia, will you let me. . . . Promise me first, that you will——'

'I'll promise, darling . . . anything you want——'

'Let me send for a doctor. . . . I implore you. . . . Well, you needn't do anything he tells you, if you like. . . . But say "yes"—only for my sake, Olyessia.'

'Oh . . . you 've caught me in a terrible trap ! No, you 'd better let me free of my promise. Even if I were really ill, dying—I wouldn't let the doctor come near me. And am I ill now ? It 's only fright that brought it on ;

it will go off when the evening comes. If it doesn't, granny will give an infusion of lilies or make some raspberry-tea. What 's the good of the doctor ? You—you 're my best doctor. You 've only just come—and I feel better already. . . . Ah, there 's only one thing wrong, I want to look at you, even if it were only with one eye, but I 'm afraid. . . .'

With a gentle effort I lifted Olyessia's head from the pillow. Her face blazed with feverish redness ; her dark eyes shone unnaturally bright ; her dry lips trembled nervously. Long, red scratches ploughed her forehead, cheeks, and neck. There were dark bruises on her forehead and under her eyes.

'Don't look at me. . . . I implore you. . . . I 'm ugly now,' Olyessia besought me in a whisper, trying to cover my eyes with her hand.

My heart overflowed with pity. I nestled my lips on Olyessia's hand, which lay motionless on the blanket, and began to cover it with long, quiet kisses. In the time before I used to kiss her hands too, but she always would draw them away from me in hasty, bashful fright. But now she made no resistance to my caress and with her other hand she gently smoothed my hair.

'You know it all ?' she asked in a whisper.

I bent my head in silence. It is true I had not understood everything from Nikita Nazarich's story. Only I did not want Olyessia to be agitated by having to recall the events of the morning. Suddenly a wave of irrepressible fury overwhelmed me at the idea of the outrage to which she had been subjected.

'Oh, why wasn't I there!' I cried, holding myself straight and clenching my fists. 'I would . . . I would have——'

'Well, don't worry . . . don't worry. . . . Don't be angry, darling. . . .' Olyessia interrupted me meekly.

I could not keep back the tears any more which had been choking my throat and burning my eyes. I pressed my face close to Olyessia's shoulder, and I began to cry bitterly, silently, trembling all over my body.

'You are crying? You are crying?' There was surprise, tenderness, and compassion in her voice. 'My darling . . . don't . . . please don't. . . . Don't torment yourself, my darling. . . . I feel so happy near you. . . . Don't let us cry while we are together. Let us be happy for the last days, then it won't be so hard for us to part.'

I raised my head in amazement. A vague presentiment began slowly to press upon my heart.

'The last days, Olyessia? What do you mean—the last? Why should we part?'

Olyessia shut her eyes and kept silence for some seconds. 'We must part, Vanichka,' she said resolutely. 'When I'm a little bit better, we'll go away from here, granny and I. We must not stay here any longer.'

'Are you afraid of anything?'

'No, my darling, I'm not afraid of anything,

if it comes to that. But why should I tempt people into mischief? Perhaps you don't know. . . . Over there—in Perebrod. . . . I was so angry and ashamed that I threatened them. . . . And now if anything happens, they will inform on us. If the cattle begin to die or a hut is set on fire—we shall be the guilty ones. Granny'—she turned to Manuilikha, raising her voice—'isn't it true what I say?'

'What did you say, little granddaughter? I confess I didn't hear,' the old woman mumbled, coming closer and putting her hand to her ear.

'I said that whatever misfortune happens in Perebrod now they 'll put all the blame on us.'

'That 's true, that 's true, Olyessia—they 'll throw everything on us, the miserable wretches. . . . We are no dwellers in this world. They will destroy us both, destroy us utterly, the cursed. . . . Besides, how did they drive me out of the village? . . . Why? . . . Wasn't it just the same? I threatened them . . . just out of vexation, too. . . . One stupid fool of a woman—and lo and behold her child died. It was no fault of mine at all—not a dream of my dreaming or a spirit of my calling; but they nearly killed me all the same, the devils. . . . They began to stone me. . . . I ran away and only just managed to protect you—you were a little tiny child then. . . . Well, I thought, it doesn't matter if they give it to me, but why should an innocent child be injured. . . . No, it all comes to the same thing—they 're savages, a dirty lot of gallows'-birds.'

'But where will you go? You haven't any relations or friends anywhere. . . . Finally, you'll have to have money to settle in a new place.'

'We'll make shift somehow,' Olyessia said negligently. 'There'll be money as well. Granny has saved something.'

'Money as well!' the old woman echoed angrily, going away from the bed. 'Widows' mites, washed in tears——'

'Olyessia. . . . What's to become of me? You don't want even to think of me!' I exclaimed, feeling a bitter, sick, ugly reproach against Olyessia rising within me.

She raised herself a little, and, careless of her grandmother's presence, took my head into her hands, and kissed me on the cheeks and forehead several times in succession.

'I think of you most of all, my own! Only . . . you see . . . it's not our fate to be together . . . that is it. . . . You remember, I spread out the cards for you? Everything happened as they foretold. It means that Fate does not will our happiness. . . . If it were not for this, do you think I would be frightened of anything?'

'Olyessia, you're talking of fate again!' I cried impatiently. 'I don't want to believe in it . . . and I never will believe.'

'Oh no, no, no! . . . Don't say that.' Olyessia began in a frightened whisper. 'It's not for me I'm afraid, but you. No you'd better not start us talking about it.'

In vain I tried to dissuade Olyessia; in vain

I painted glowing pictures of unbroken happiness for her, which neither curious fate nor ugly, wicked people could disturb. Olyessia only kissed my hands and shook her head.

'No . . . no . . . no. . . . I know. I see,' she repeated persistently. 'There 's nothing but sorrow awaits us . . . nothing . . . nothing.'

Disconcerted and baffled by this superstitious obstinacy, I asked at length, 'At least you will let me know the day you are going away ?'

Olyessia pondered. Suddenly the shadow of a smile flickered over her lips. 'I 'll tell you a little story for that. Once upon a time a wolf was running through the forest when he saw a little hare and said to him : "Hi, you hare ! I 'll eat you !" The hare began to implore him : "Have mercy on me. I want to live. I have little children at home." The wolf did not agree, so the hare said : "Well, let me live another three days in the world ; then you can eat me, but still I shall feel it easier to die." The wolf gave him his three days. He didn't eat him, but only kept a watch on him. One day passed, then the second, and at last the third was coming to an end. "Well, get ready now," said the wolf, "I 'm going to eat you at once." Then my hare began to weep with bitter tears. "Oh, why did you give me those three days, wolf ? It would have been far better if you had eaten the first moment that you saw me. The whole of these three days it hasn't been life for me, but torment."

'Darling, that little hare spoke the truth. Don't you think so?'

I was silent, distraught by an anxious foreboding of the loneliness that threatened me. Olyessia suddenly raised herself and sat up in bed. Her face grew serious at once. 'Listen, Vanya . . .' she said slowly. 'Tell me, were you happy while you were with me? Did you feel that it was good?'

'Olyessia! Can you still ask?'

'Wait. . . . Did you regret having met me? Were you thinking of another woman while you were with me?'

'Never for one single second! Not only when I was with you, but when I was alone, I never had a thought for any one but you.'

'Were you jealous of me? Were you ever angry with me? Were you ever wretched when you were with me?'

'Never, Olyessia, never!'

She put both her hands upon my shoulders, and looked into my eyes with love indescribable.

'Then I tell you, my darling, that you will never think evilly or sadly of me when you remember me,' she said with conviction, as though she were reading the future in my eyes. 'When we part you will be miserable, terribly miserable. . . . You will cry, you will not find a place to rest anywhere. And then everything will pass and fade away, and you will think of me without sorrow, easily and happily.'

She let her head fall back on the pillows again and whispered in a feeble voice:

'Now go, my darling. . . . Go home, my precious. . . . I am a little bit tired. No, wait . . . kiss me. . . . Don't be frightened of granny . . . she won't mind. You don't mind, do you, granny ? '

'Say good-bye. Part, as you should,' the old woman muttered in discontent. . . . 'Why should you want to hide from me ? I 've known it a long while.'

'Kiss me here and here . . . and here,' Olyessia said, touching her eyes, cheeks and mouth with her fingers.

'Olyessia, you 're saying good-bye to me as though we shall never see each other again ! ' I cried in terror.

'I don't know, I don't know, my darling. I don't know anything. Now, go and God be with you. No, wait . . . just one little moment more. . . . Bend down to me. . . . You know what I regret ? ' she began to whisper, touching my cheeks with her lips. 'That you haven't given me a child. . . . Oh, how happy I should be ! '

I went out into the passage, escorted by Manuilikha. Half the heaven was covered by a black cloud with sharp, curly edges, but the sun was still shining, bending to the east. There was something ominous in this mixing of light and oncoming darkness. The old woman looked up, shading her eyes with her hand as it were an umbrella, and shook her head meaningly.

'There 'll be a thunderstorm over Perebrod, to-day,' she said with conviction. 'And hail as well, most likely.'

XIV

I HAD almost reached Perebrod when a sudden whirlwind rose, driving columns of dust before it on the road. The first heavy, scattered drops of rain began to fall.

Manuilikha was not mistaken. The storm which had been gathering all through the insufferable heat of the day burst with extraordinary force over Perebrod. The lightning flashed almost without intermission, and the window panes of my room trembled and rang with the roll of the thunder. At about eight o'clock in the evening the storm abated for some minutes, but only to begin again with new exasperation. Suddenly something poured down on to the roof with a deafening crash, and on to the walls of the old house. I rushed to the window. Huge hailstones, as big as a walnut, were falling furiously on to the earth and bouncing high in the air again. I glanced at the mulberry bush which grew against the house. It stood quite bare; every leaf had been beaten off by the blows of the awful hail. Beneath the window appeared Yarmola's figure, hardly visible in the darkness. He had covered his head in his sheepskin and run out of the kitchen to close the shutters. But he was too late. A huge piece of ice suddenly struck one of the windows with such force that it was smashed, and the tinkling splinters of glass were scattered over the floor of the room.

A fatigue came over me, and I lay down on the bed in my clothes. I thought I would never be able to sleep at all that night, but would toss from side to side in impotent anguish until the morning. So I decided it would be better not to undress ; later I might be able to tire myself if only a little by walking up and down the room, over and over again. But a strange thing happened to me. It seemed to me that I had shut my eyes only a second ; but when I opened them, long, bright sunbeams were already stretching through the chinks of the shutters, and innumerable motes of golden dust were turning round and round within them.

Yarmola was standing over my bed. On his face was written stern anxiety and impatient expectation. Probably he had been waiting long for me to wake.

'Sir,' he said in a dull voice, in which one could distinguish his uneasiness. 'You 'd better go away from here, sir.'

I put my feet out of bed and looked at Yarmola with amazement. 'Better go away ? Where to ? Why ? You 're mad, surely.'

'No, I 'm not mad,' Yarmola snarled. 'You didn't hear what happened through yesterday's hail ? Half the corn of the village is like as though it had been trodden underfoot—cripple Maxim's, the Goat's, old Addlepate's, the brothers Prokopchuk's, Gordi Olefir's. . . . She put the mischief on us, the devilish witch. . . . May she rot in hell ! '

In an instant I remember what had happened yesterday, the threat Olyessia had made by the church, and her apprehensions.

' And all the village is in a riot now,' Yarmola continued. ' They got drunk first thing in the morning, and now they 're fighting. . . . They 've got something bad to say of you, too, sir. . . . You know what our people are like ? . . . If they do something to the witches, that won't matter, it 'll serve 'em to rights ; but you, sir—I 'll just say this one word of warning, you get out of here as quick as you can.'

So Olyessia's fears had come true. I must let her know at once of the danger that threatened her and Manuilikha. I got up hurriedly, rinsed my face without ever standing still, and in half an hour I was riding full gallop towards the Devil's Corner.

The nearer I came to the chicken-legged hut the stronger grew the vague melancholy anxiety within me. I said to myself that in a moment a new, unexpected misfortune would certainly befall me.

I almost galloped over the narrow footpath that wound up the sandy hill. The windows of the hut were open, the door wide.

' My God, what has happened ? ' I whispered, and my heart sank as I entered the passage.

The hut was empty. Over it all reigned the sad, dirty disorder that always remains after a hurried departure. Heaps of dust and rags lay about the floor, and the wooden frame of a bed stood in the corner.

My heart was utterly sad, overflowing with tears; I wanted to get out of the hut already, when my eye was caught by something bright, hung, as if on purpose, in a corner of the window-frame. It was a string of the cheap red beads which they call 'corals' in Polyessie—the only thing that remained to me in memory of Olyessia and her tender, great-hearted love.

www.ingramcontent.com/pod-product-compliance
Lightning Source LLC
LaVergne TN
LVHW030910080826
845145LV00010B/2837

* 9 7 8 1 4 1 0 1 0 5 6 8 4 *